MW01178259

I am Kasper Klotz

I am Kasper Klotz

a novel

Sky Gilbert

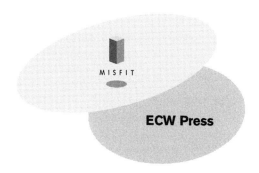

MISFIT

ECW Press

NATIONAL LIBRARY OF CANADA CATALOGUING IN PUBLICATION DATA

Gilbert, Sky
I am Kasper Klotz

"A misFit book".
ISBN 1-55022-477-8

I. Title.

PS8563.I4744312 2001   C813'.54   C2001-900817-1
PR9199.3.G524812 2001

Edited by Michael Holmes / a misFit book
Cover and text design by Tania Craan
Cover images by Andrew Syred / Stone, Monica Vinella / Photonica
Layout by Wiesia Kolasinska

Printed by AGMV

Distributed in Canada by
General Distribution Services,
325 Humber College Blvd.,
Toronto, ON M9W 7C3

Published by ECW PRESS
2120 Queen Street East, Suite 200
Toronto, ON M4E 1E2
ecwpress.com

This book is set in Minion.

PRINTED AND BOUND IN CANADA

The publication of *Kasper Klotz* has been generously supported by the Canada Council, the Ontario Arts Council and the Government of Canada through the Book Publishing Industry Development Program. Canadä

Acknowledgements

This is a work of fiction. The characters, thoughts and ideas in this book come from my imagination. Nevertheless, several people have inspired me. Specifically, I would like to thank Michael Ellner, Rob Johnston, Christine Maggiore, Carl Strygg, and Ian Young for their brilliance. And their courage.

for Ian Jarvis

It is my contention that this mechanism of "killing of the shamed" is one of the most powerful, though deeply repressed, dynamics of the AIDS epidemic: that which is enacted in real murder in tribal culture becomes a more sublimated but nevertheless equally venomous outpouring of death wishes towards drug addicts and homosexuals.

— Casper G. Schmidt, "The Group-Fantasy Origins of Aids"

I AM KASPER KLOTZ. My name has been changed to protect the innocent. I understand that you hate me. That's okay. I was meant to be hated. You were meant to hate. You needed someone to hate. So here I am. Really, I don't mind. I kind of like it. I am your worst nightmare. I am your every waking dread. I am the bad man who comes and gets you. Am I giving you the creeps right now? Are you pulling the covers up? Good. I like that. I know you like that too.

It's not as if I'm some sort of monster. No, I'm human. That's the amazing thing about me — I'm human. I resemble you (vaguely). But you do find me ugly and disgusting. Which is only natural because I'm evil. I do bad things. What bad things?

You'll find out.

Actually, I'll tell you now.

I kill people. Innocent people. I make them die. But first they have to really know about their deaths. They have to see their deaths before them. They have to quiver and beg for forgiveness.

And then I kill them.

Making them very afraid gives me pleasure.

You see, there's something you've got (unless you're incredibly stupid), and that's . . . what? Well, it's a deeply ingrained fear of losing your consciousness. Sure, you might have the odd drink now and then. Who doesn't like a cocktail at the end of the day? Just to, you know, wind down? Not ten cocktails or anything. Just one. Just one measly cocktail! All right? But what's really scary for you is to imagine that your consciousness has stopped.

There. You're not reading this anymore. Ha ha. You're dead. Someone else's consciousness is taking over.

I used to have a friend. He's dead now. (I had so many, they're all dead now.) He was an obsessive-compulsive. Every day he'd ask me "Is there life after death?" Every day, for a while, I'd give him a reassuring answer. You see, it was part of his neurosis, he couldn't stop thinking about death. He needed someone to tell him there was life after death because, being nuts, he needed to have a clear reason for living. And if he believed it was all for nothing (you just die, and it's over), then he couldn't justify normal things. Such as shopping. There'd have been no more shopping for Andy if he'd decided death is final. If death is absolute, then why get up at all? Sometimes Andy didn't get up at all. I mean, why bother?

For the longest time, I was Andy's friend and confidant. Andy would come by for tea and sympathy, and I'd give them to him. Lies. All the lies.

"Oh," I'd say, "I'm a painter. I'm a real artist, and I find as an artist (yuck) that I'm tuned in to something else. Some higher power. I couldn't paint if I didn't believe in the collective unconscious. It's where my visual imagination comes from."

"Like it's dictated?" he'd ask.

"Sort of," I'd say, lying.

But Andy wouldn't be satisfied with that. We'd then have to talk about the collective unconscious.

"So what's the collective unconscious?" he'd ask. "Is that where I'll go after death?"

"I think so," I'd say.

"But will I still be *me* after death? Will I still be *Andy*?"

"Why, sure," I'd say (lying again, actually yearning for the moment when I could hit him all at once with the bitter truth. But not then). "You'll still be Andy, but you'll be part of something larger and more amazing."

"I don't know if I want to be part of something 'larger and more amazing,' I just want to be *Andy*."

"It won't be so bad," I'd say.

And that would sort of make him happy. Until the next day's question.

Anyway, this little question-and-answer thing went on every day over tea for years. Until I couldn't stand it anymore. I got really tired of supporting Andy's stupid obsessive-compulsive delusions. I became tired of his dumb little questions. I grew tired of his whole routine. Besides, I knew it would be a lot of fun making him feel really bad. I mean, people are dying every day in Africa, for God's sake. Protestants got tortured and ripped apart by the Spanish fucking Inquisition in the Dark Ages. And none of those poor sods had any of Andy's bountiful, bourgeois, white-boy, middle-class time to worry about life after death. Or, pardon me, life after death that was, well, fun and recognizable for Andy. So one day I just turned on him.

"Is there life after death?" asked Andy, putting on this cute little-boy pout that always used to get him so well laid at the baths.

I took a sip of my tea. Then I had at him. "No, Andy," I said. "There is no fucking life after death. When you die, it's over. Nada, nothing. You're dead. That's it. No merging, no miasma. No God, no heaven, no hell. Your fucking stupid little *Andy* consciousness stops, and that's a horror that you can't imagine. Because you'll never live it, because you'll no longer be *Andy*. And your life has no meaning. Absolutely no meaning. There is no pattern, no hope. This world is a tiny speck in a huge malignant universe. No one cares if you live or die, Andy. And you will die eventually. Maybe tomorrow. After a while, there will be nothing left — not even a memory. And what's a memory, after all? So if you need this kind of stupid reassurance and these idiotic lies to give you the courage to get out of bed in the morning, then I'd say just don't do it. Just don't bother to get up."

"But what about what you said before?" He was actually whimpering now. "What about being an artist and feeling you are tapped into some sort of collective unconscious?"

"That was all crap. I just told you that to shut you up. I'm a fucking painter because I'm a lot cleverer than almost everybody in this goddamned world, and I'm just fucking bored, and I have to do something with my mornings after you come over for tea."

"But — "

"No buts, Andy. When it's over, it's over. So if I were you, I'd go and screw your brains out tonight. Because you'll be dead soon. Probably because of AIDS. So have a lot of fun when you're fucking conscious, because you won't be fucking conscious long."

It was very awkward after that. My friendship with Andy the obsessive-compulsive was never quite the same.

Why You Hate Me

1. BECAUSE I KILL PEOPLE. Well, that should be pretty fucking obvious. Most people aren't too fond of a murderer. Even though the people I kill completely deserve it and bring it on themselves.

2. BECAUSE I TELL MY VICTIMS WHAT I'M GOING TO DO. Yeah, I'd say this makes you even madder. It's one thing to go around killing people, it's another thing to look someone in the eye and say, "Hey, you're going to die." That's one thing people really don't like. I don't understand it, what's the big deal?

I'll admit there's not much thrill in killing other artists. A lot of them are already completely into death and dying because their art is all about that morbid stuff. The same goes for lower-class types, who just don't have the money to keep death away. For them, disease and death are just normal parts of everyday life.

But middle-class people are fun to kill. "I'm murdering you," I say. "You're going to die." This completely freaks out the suburban types. After all, their lives are devoted to staying alive, to ignoring death. That's why they always keep the suburban streets clean and free of "homeless" types. They don't want to be reminded that *life is short and painful.* Yeah, killing the middle classes is great. It's fun to see the terror in their eyes as they confront death for the first time in their stupid, corny, pointless, cowardly lives.

3. BECAUSE I LOOK, WELL, DIFFERENT THAN YOU. That's always a problem, isn't it? I'm not pretty. I'm big and ugly. Everything I own is in bad taste. And I smell. And I'm a bit effeminate, which definitely doesn't go with my shaved head. I wear army pants, and I have disgusting tattoos. If I were a nice, clean-looking murderer, then you wouldn't hate me so much.

4. BECAUSE YOU LIKE HATING SOMEONE. It's all very well for you to deny this. I know, you're a very loving person, and you're into having warm feelings about everyone. Crap! You gossip about your friends. You tell dirt about the people closest to you. You're very competitive, and you feel really inadequate. (I don't know — it could be sex, it could be your job or lack of one, it could be anything.) And the only way you feel better is by nurturing nasty feelings about others. I'm a repository for all your jealousy and fear. "It's Kasper's fault." "Isn't Kasper ugly and horrible and evil, don't you just hate him?" Go on, hate me. If I didn't exist, then you would have created me. Actually, you did, didn't you? But God knows you don't want to admit that you hate yourselves. That would be too honest. So choose me instead. Go on, spill it all on me. You'll feel a lot better.

My Neighbours

Okay, enough about you. Let's talk about me. Me and my hate. You know, one of the things I hate most is my neighbours. My fucking stupid, pitiful, gay, AIDS-infected neighbours.

I live in an apartment building in the middle of the gay ghetto. Ghetto's a great name for it. It truly is.

Here's an AIDS joke for you.

Q: "What does gay stand for?"

A: "Got AIDS yet?"

Sometimes it seems like everyone's just waiting to get it or trying to get it or weeping about having just got it. My apartment building is the saddest thing on four posts stuck in the mud. Really. People jokingly call it the "drag queen apartment building," which is too true, because it's mostly filled with "female impersonators," as they like to be called. Actually, it's filled with funny-looking gay men whose only hope of being attractive is to dress up like women. That's sad, isn't it? I mean, it's one thing if you're a good-looking masculine guy and like to put on a dress just to be silly. The guys in my building are seriously challenged in the attractiveness department, such flaming cases they can barely pass for guys. One of them, I swear, when he's out of drag, just looks like an extremely effeminate balding bank teller. Then, when he puts on a dress, he becomes, well, almost appealing.

You see, I'm not denying these gals are kind of cute when they get all dolled up. But when they take off their sparkling duds, their lives are dismal. They're bank tellers, or they sweep the floor of the pharmacy next door. And they're all dying of AIDS, I swear, all of them.

I gave it to at least three of these Judy Garland wannabes, I really did. I am so proud of myself — they totally wanted it and deserved it (well, at least two of them did). So I'm glad they've got it, and I'm really proud to have given it to them.

I want you to get to know my fabulously annoying "victims."

Of course, I've changed the names to protect the innocent, so I'll call one "Nick," one "Alphonse," and the other — the hands-down winner of them all — "Whiny Betty."

Nick lives on one side of me, and Whiny Betty lives on the other, and Alphonse lives below us. (The Crown Fucking Prince of the Imperial Court of Russia lives down the hall.) Alphonse isn't annoying at all except that he's such a fucking saint. Nick, Whiny Betty, and the Crown Prince — who wouldn't want to kill them?

Okay, let's start with Whiny Betty. She's certainly the most eternally annoying of the bunch.

First, she's ugly. She's a thirty-four-year-old, much-too-skinny, balding, AIDS-infected faggot. So what else is new?

Second, she's got a horrible dog. It's fat and yappy, and she just loves it to death. When she walks her dog, she's very annoying. She goes around holding her little plastic poop bag like she's the queen of fucking England. She wears this perpetual sneer as if everything smells bad. (Except for the dog shit, which she seems to just love collecting from her little "Snuggles." Yeah, the overweight Corgi is actually called Snuggles.)

Third, she has no life except for her drag acts and the nights she spends with her legs in the air at the baths. She works at the pharmacy and claims she stocks the shelves. But every time I've seen her there, she wasn't stocking the shelves. I've only seen her cleaning the floor. She enjoys not being quite as sick as all the dying AIDS cases who come in to buy their expensive, lethal drugs. She enjoys helping the unfortunate — that's her big thing.

Her drag act is terrible. She tries to do this bitchy queen number. Her character is called "Elvita." God knows why. Somewhere between Elvira, Mistress of the Dark and a popular cheese spread. And like so many drag queens, she has this elevated concept of herself that is totally unrelated to reality. She thinks she's incredibly biting and cutting and witty and on the edge. She's not. She's really boring. She tries to trade carps and quips with the audience, but whenever she performs it's very disappointing. Again like so many drag queens, she makes up for what she lacks in talent with a huge serving of "compassion."

Elvita is the queen of all the AIDS-benefit performers. Her whole drag life is like one big benefit number. What does she perform? Well, she's manipulated a couple of her friends (who are *slightly* more talented than she is but still nothing special) into doing this act called The Booboos. They lip-synch to 1970s songs while wearing appalling 1970s outfits. (All right, the songs might not be so bad if someone else was lip-synching to them.) The Booboos are always performing to raise money for some AIDS hospice, for local AIDS organizations, or just to grant some poor fag's dying wish to go to Mexico and fuck his brains out before he dies. Everything they do is for AIDS. Which I think is pointless and stupid. But even if I didn't think it's hopeless to raise money for stupid AIDS organizations, I'd still find the way Elvita harps about her incredibly generous heart too much to take. You see, each time she manages to raise a little money for some dumb AIDS cause (which is every time she performs), she just *has* to say a few words about all the good work she is doing. She used to do it in the guise of coming out after the act and saying, "So, up to this point this year, I've managed to raise $1,500 for AIDS causes." Everyone would clap, of course. They always do. Just *mention* AIDS to most fags and they get very teary and mushy. And then they clap. They clap for the clap. But as Elvita has become increasingly enamoured of her own good works, and as she has begun to realize that she isn't very talented (or loved for her actual performances), the speeches have become more and more embarrassing. These days she comes out and starts a sort of eulogy for herself, always mentioning she is HIV positive. The audience is hushed, of course. With one of the other Booboos at her side, she asks, "How long have I been working for 'the cause,' Anita?"

Anita says, "Going on three years, Elvita."

"And sometimes I've had to stop because of my own illnesses, isn't that right, Anita?"

"Yes, Elvita."

Of course, Elvita doesn't need fat old Anita up there at all except to have someone to hurl these rhetorical questions at, and, because the audience enjoys this maudlin display, Anita chums along. Before the edifying spectacle is over, Elvita launches into a tearful speech (yes, sometimes she cries) in which she remembers all her dead friends and all the money she's made for "the cause." She ends, of course, on her own incredible generosity and her courage in fighting her own terrible disease. Let me tell you, even if there's only one fucking drunk left in the bar, Elvita will do her self-serving mawkish monologue one more time, and that lonely old rubby will put his pasty arthritic hands together and clap for her. Because how can people in the gay community resist? God help them if they refuse to clap for Elvita. God help them if they don't applaud for AIDS.

When it comes to her personal life and AIDS, we find the "inner" Elvita, whom I call Whiny Betty. She lives in an infinitesimal apartment filled to the brim with antiques (junk). There are pictures of her family everywhere. Betty is very big on family. She comes from some small town, and her family is an incredibly ugly bunch of people (almost deformed, actually). She has a sister and a mother whom she really loves. And before she came down with HIV or AIDS (or whatever the fuck she's got), she wasn't very popular with her family because they thought she was an evil homosexual. She couldn't get her family to come out for Gay Pride or anything. And they were always asking her accusing questions about her lifestyle. Then, when Betty invited them all over for dinner and tearfully informed them she was HIV positive, they all suddenly started loving her again. I even saw Betty's sad old lower-class dad at the last Gay Pride Parade.

Now Betty is one of those gals who, a few years after AIDS emerged, fought like crazy to get a positive diagnosis. It's not that she fought to get "infected" — that was kind of an accident, to put it politely. No, I saw Betty around before she started boasting about her diagnosis, and I could tell she was cruising for a death sentence. For Betty, it's all about getting the pity vote. *Without HIV, she was, by day, a janitor at a pharmacy and, by night, an ugly untalented drag queen whose family despised her. With HIV, she became a glamorous drag star whose family visited her at least once a month to keep up on her precarious health.*

Except that, as far as I know, Betty's never actually been sick.

You see, when she went for her AIDS test, she really had to try hard to get a positive result. She went back again and again. Not because she had symptoms — there was never anything wrong. Okay, she always had a handkerchief stuck into her sleeve and a red nose. And she complained of frequent colds, the usual aches and pains. At first, there were dire observations such as "It's weird. I'm getting so many colds. . . . I wonder why that is?" Then they became "I just don't feel right, I think I should get The Test." I'd meet her on the street; she'd be all worried-looking, on her way to the doctor. But the results would always come back indeterminate. And she'd say, "Indeterminate . . . that's a very bad sign. I think I should get tested again in a month." And I could tell. She was wishing, praying, and hoping that her stubborn "indeterminate" would become HIV positive.

So I decided to take the matter into my own hands. At the time, I didn't know Betty very well. I could hear her stereo through the wall, usually when she was practising some drag number in her cha-cha heels. Sometimes I thought I heard crying sounds. That was about it.

Now, you see, the thing is, Betty had actually sucked on my fabulous cock once. And I thought it was time to remind her of that ominous fact. I thought it was time for death to knock on her door.

So I did one grey March afternoon. You know, one of those days when the weather has been "indeterminate" for so long you kind of wish it would just snow and be winter again. Something. Anything.

Betty was in the middle of rehearsing "You Gotta Have a Gimmick." Of course, she was going to be the girl with a horn. I think I just decided to kill her off because I couldn't stand listening to that damn number through the paper-thin wall of that fucking apartment building anymore.

She looked awful. Her long ugly hair was pulled up in a kind of bandana — which was supposed to look like a casual attempt to keep her hair out of her eyes — à la Cyd Charisse on break at MGM. But she didn't look anything at all like Cyd. I told her that I had something important to say to her.

And then I gave her the news.

Betty was so sure she had AIDS because (like everyone else in the damned gay world) she'd spent so many nights being such a dedicated slut. A confirmed bottom, every night Betty had been at the baths with her ass in the air. I will say one thing about her, she had a great ass. Very round and high and a bit furry. Just the way I like 'em. Which is how I ended up fucking her. I fucked her years ago, at the baths, before anybody started using condoms seriously. When Betty was an almost cute kid — she was never actually cute. She knew she'd been a slut. She still was, the dumb little fuck. And because she was such a drunken piece of work at night, she never really got acquainted with the guys she had sex with. A lot of gay guys are like that. They get drunk because they want to have sex, but they don't want to know who their partners are. Why? Because they might meet them on the street the next day and feel obligated to say hi.

So Betty was a sluttish bottom whose butt I had once fucked. This put me in a pretty fabulous position from which to give a death sentence. Besides, as I said, I really didn't want to hear "You Gotta Have a Gimmick" again.

"Bart," I said (Betty's real name was Bart), "I've got something to tell you."

"What?" asked Betty. She looked really pitiful. Ripe for the reaper.

And just like when I told Andy there is no life after death, the whole thing was simply irresistible. I acted as though it was all very difficult for me to say. "Listen, Bart, I don't know you very well."

"But we're neighbours."

"Yeah, we're neighbours."

"And I think I've seen you at my shows."

"Yeah, I think I've been at one or two."

"So what is it? Is the music too loud?"

"No, Bart, no, it's just, well, this is kind of tough for me to say."

"Hey, Kasper, you're scaring me."

"Sorry, but. . . ." I looked at her really pitifully. "It is kinda scary."

"Oh, no, what is it? You're not . . . sick?" Whiny Betty put on her best sympathetic face. She had a few.

"No, I've never been sick a day in my life. But I noticed that you've been sniffling a lot lately." I had to stop myself from saying "snivelling." Well, that got her going.

"Yes, I'm going through a tough time. Frequent colds. And, you know . . . the colds go on and on. They just won't stop. I start worrying, but then I figure there are a lot more worse off than me. And my test is still indeterminate, so I figure I'll just cross my fingers."

"That's what I came to talk to you about."

"What do you mean?"

"Listen, Bart, I've been your neighbour for a long time, and for a long time I've known something that, well, it might upset you. But I figure it's best to lay it on the line. To be honest. To tell the truth." (I used "I figure" because I thought it sounded sincere. It worked.)

"What are you trying to say?"

"I came here to tell you, well, I thought you should know. . . ." I looked down, pitiful and ashamed. "I'm HIV positive."

"Oh, no, Kasper, that's terrible." Betty took a Kleenex from her sleeve and blew her nose. "I'm so sorry. When did you find out?"

"Oh, I've known for a while."

"My heart goes out to you, Kasper. I'll put you in my prayers every night." Betty went and picked up a nauseating stuffed bear lying on her junky faux antique bed. "Every night I say prayers for all my HIV-positive friends. The list is getting kind of long. But I'll add you. I don't mind."

Yeah, she's a fucking saint, that Whiny Betty.

"That's just it, you see, Bart, I. . . ." I was going to get an Oscar for this one. I turned away, tortured.

"What is it?"

"The thing is, Bart, my doctor told me I should be sure to tell everyone I had sex with, and — "

"Kasper, you don't mean? . . ."

"Yes, Bart." I turned for dramatic effect. I'd managed to get my eyes sort of teary, and I knew they'd kick-start Betty's waterworks. "I have to tell you that we were. . . ." I pretended to be shy and inarticulate talking about sex. "Sexually intimate a few years ago. And I've been HIV positive for a while, so I thought you should know. I'm sorry, Bart. I'm . . . I'm sorry. I might have . . . I might have given it to you."

Bart totally bought it. He bought the awkwardness, the prudishness. I was playing the "I'm so ashamed I've got AIDS" act I'd seen in countless made-for-TV movies. It was great.

"But, Kasper, I don't remember. . . ." He acted as if he was in denial.

But I thought I could see a ray of hope somewhere behind his eyes. This news would give his life new meaning. "Well, it was one night at, well, a place I don't go very often. The spa on Bunting."

"The spa on Bunting?"

"Yes."

"Oh, my God. I've been there once or twice." Who did he think he was kidding? He was there every fucking night. "My God, Kasper. Kasper. . . ."

He reached out his arms. He wanted to hug me. Jesus, he was so ugly. But I knew I had to, so I hugged him, and he started to cry. He let it all out. The yearning. His need to be special. His separation from his family. It could all come out now because he was going to be HIV positive. He was going to be one of the chosen.

I comforted him for a while, and then I just had to go. I pretended I was too overwhelmed with emotion. As I was leaving, I noticed he was a huge mess. I knew he'd get right on the phone and call all of his friends to tell them the special, melodramatic news.

For a while, he avoided me. Then one day, about two weeks later, he came up to me on the street and said, "Kasper, I just wanted to tell you, well, I tested positive." He looked brave, and his eyes glistened.

I looked down, shyly. "I'm sorry, Bart," I said.

He hugged me. I could feel his naked body under his spring coat. His chest had absolutely no definition.

"Don't be sorry. It all happened before safe sex. How could you know?" And then he marched off, bravely, with his fat little dog.

You know, killing Whiny Betty has been a pleasure, almost a public service. Now she cries through the walls every night. When she's not out getting fucked at the baths. She cries about her pitiful plight, a lonely AIDS-infected drag queen. The whole thing makes me laugh.

First Prison Letter from
Cindy Lou Williams

Dear Mr. Klotz,

How are you? I am fine. I'm starting my letter like that because that's how I always used to write to my cousin. My slightly older cousin Maggie, who is all grown up and lives in Maine now. When she was a child, she used to get overexcited and jump up and down and shake her hands on her loose little wrists.

I probably shouldn't be writing to you. In fact, it would probably kill my dear mother if she found out. But I'm certainly not going to tell her.

I mean, it could be because I'm your typical small-town spinster and you're a big burly prisoner soon to be on trial for attempted murder.

Or it could just be because I want to. I've always been interested in the nature of evil. I still teach Sunday school. What else is there for me to do on Sundays — giggle — so that's what I do!

If you saw me, it would make you laugh. I am thirty-five years old and tragically destined to remain unmarried. There is something about my face which is not and will never be pretty. We all have our cross to bear.

You know, I feel sorry for the boy you tried to kill. And all the others (I hear there are others). But when I looked into your big brown eyes, I thought, there's an intelligent person. And I thought that you would have a good reason. And you should share that reason with a sympathetic ear.

Aren't you a painter? Didn't you paint dirty paintings? I tried to find a book about your paintings at the library, but the librarian looked at me very strangely, more strangely than usual, so I have the feeling that what you have painted must be very bad. It should probably be censored.

There's nothing much to tell about my life, Mr. Klotz, except to say that I will be attending your trial every day. The judge is a fine man, and he is definitely an upstanding citizen. The jury is certainly made up of a serious-looking group of people who are doing their duty, which is important. Jury duty is very important, I think.

One idea I had was to try to entertain you. But I don't even know if you will actually receive these letters or if you want them. You should tell me. There's no point in me casting pearls before swine. My life, frankly, hasn't had much meaning up until now. I mean, I've tried my best to be a good person. But is that enough? Of course, I've had certain unfulfilled longings, but that's very clichéd. Then I saw you in front of the courthouse. You looked a bit like Charles Laughton in *The Hunchback of Notre Dame*. A very good movie, but I don't know if they let you rent movies in there! I was moved.

Since my life is essentially anticlimactic and uneventful, perhaps you could tell me what you want to hear about. Probably the biggest event in my life is the June Bug Epidemic, which nearly killed my dear mother. You just tell me if you want to hear anymore from me at all. If not, I'll understand.

Try to be a better person. God is watching you.

Sincerely,

Cindy Lou Williams

My Neighbours

So on the one side, there's crying, whining, dying Betty. And on the other side, there's Nick. Nick MacIntosh. A big queen: part Scottish, part Greek. All trash.

Nick moved in nearly a year ago. Which means I've been in sort of a rush to kill him. But it didn't take me long to realize he's very killable.

He's a therapist. A licensed synchro-stimulation therapist. What a load. I don't know if you know anything about synchro-stimulation therapy, but it's all a scam. Most of the gay "therapists" are prostitutes. I mean, I'm sure there's one or two "real" gay synchro-stimulation therapists in the world, but basically the whole racket is a licence to touch strangers' bodies for a fee and not get arrested. The so-called theory behind synchro-stimulation is that you carry pain and stress in different parts of your body. So the therapist, if he or she touches certain parts of your body in the right way, can release the pain and stress. The gay ones are the worst. There isn't a single one who isn't giving out sex with the therapy. They'll deny it — they'll all deny it because they all want to look respectable.

Nick is one of the biggest, most revolting queens I've ever met. He's so pretentious. He has his little synchro-stimulation therapist sign framed and hung on the wall.

I first noticed him because of the horrible New Age music that started floating into my apartment. That New Age music. It can kill you. Vapidity can do you in.

Nick is the kind of fag I hate. Because of his synchro-stimulation practice and his HIV-positive status (in other words, it's partially my fault), he's been through extensive psychotherapy. This means he's a "healthy" person even though he's dying. He talks in therapy-speak, and his big thing is rising above his past. Like Whiny Betty, he comes from a small town. What's in his past exactly I don't know. All I know is I met this old lady friend of his once when I was having tea with him. And when Nick was off in the can having one of his extensive and smelly dumps (he takes protease inhibitors), this old lady turned to me and said, "Nick's done so well for himself, hasn't he?" She gestured around the room to the therapy table and his SST certificate and all his yucky knick-knacks and gewgaws.

I couldn't resist dishing out the dirt, so I said, "Well, he still has some monetary problems."

The old lady responded, "Yes, I know, but if you only knew what he has come *from*. If you only knew his *family*."

And then Nick came back from the john smiling, looking all relieved.

The way the woman spoke was so portentous I almost couldn't imagine the depravity of his family. The way she said "If you only knew his *family*" made me think his mom had been a syphilitic crack whore and his dad had eaten shit on a regular basis.

So, having come from such ignominious beginnings, it's no wonder that Nick is pretentious. His basic MO (which he got from endless therapy) is to pretend to be really kind and supportive and then put himself above everybody. That and saying "I hear you." The world, to Nick, is scum, and he is better than everyone. But he isn't going to show it. Instead, he always wears this nauseating smile.

And he's always come up to me and said, "How are you, you big handsome guy?" This is irritating because I'm so unattractive — and smelly and whatnot — that people often avoid even standing near me. "What a sweet, loving man you are!" He's said this to me in front of anybody on the street just to show how caring and adjusted he is. It's completely sickening.

Now you might think it's because I'm ugly and forbidding, or because I wear a permanent frown, that I resent any cheerful fag, just out of jealousy. No, Nick is *too* cheerful. He's like the good fairy or something. Always saying "Hi!" to people with little dogs, always chatting up the guy or gal behind the store counter. He likes to wear these huge Jesus sandals even in the middle of winter. He's such a big fat fairy that he always wears a baggy hockey shirt to cover his stomach. It doesn't work. In summer, though, he wears a macramé tank top, and you can see the whole big hairy business. Nick is "out there."

"I'm not ashamed of what I am!" he says, as if he's about to break into that corny gay song.

Yeah, Nick, but some of us could use a little shame. For those who have nauseating taste in knick-knacks, and who dress like old macramé hippies, a little shame would go a long way toward improving the rest of our lives.

As I got to know Nick, after he moved in about ten months ago, I learned he isn't quite as nice and sweet as he pretends to be. In fact, he hates everybody. He makes me look like Jesus himself. I swear, I can mention anybody in the neighbourhood, and Nick will start trashing him or her. Not fun trashing, not cute trashing — no, real spiteful stuff. And he trashes in therapy-speak. "He's very sad, a very sad person," Nick will say, sipping his herbal tea with his big hairy synchro-stimulator therapist hands. "He's got issues. I don't want to go into them all now, but I will say this: there's a no self-esteem situation going on there." Or "Oh, she's very destructive. She's on a self-hating highway straight to self-destruction, and there's no turning back. I won't have anything to do with people like her. I did, once, but now I can't be bothered with them. I suggested she come in for therapy . . . but she wasn't interested. . . . It's so sad. . . ." And then he'll smile.

And I'll think, "Right on, you won't have anything to do with destructive people, but you're having tea with a killer. With the guy who's responsible for killing you. Nice try at being intelligent and respectable and having self-esteem, Nick, but it's not going to work."

How did I infect Nick? It was easy. He wanted it so bad. Not like Whiny Betty. She pretended to dread AIDS. Nick wanted to die and was very open about it.

When he first moved into the building, he was still in synchro-stimulation therapy school. All the little resident queens wanted to know who this new big queen was. So I went over for a visit, and we chatted. I told him I was a painter, which really impressed him and seemed to make up for the fact that I'm physically repulsive. Nick was already doing a bit of synchro-stimulation therapy work, and he was pretty frank about the job. He said a lot of his clients wanted him to wank them off. At least the old and ugly ones. It was the opposite situation with his younger clients. He was always trying to wank them off — to relieve their "stress points." He said he wouldn't wank off the old guys (he had his "standards"), but at the end of the "session" he'd usually give them ten minutes in the room by themselves. If they wanted to wank off, it was none of his business.

Nick also told me about all the cute boy clients he had. The ones with perfect bodies. At the time, he was dating one of them. Or chasing one of them. Whatever. So I figured, if he's dating one of his boyish synchro-stimulation therapy clients, then with the old ones it must be a hooker situation.

Well, during these early chats, he went on about what a top he was. Which made sense. Because he must have weighed 250 pounds. All of it packed into a five-foot-nine frame. He looked like an effeminate football tackle, and his face was round and pudgy like a balled-up fist. I could tell he had a big dick. So I was sure some of his older clients wanted him to fuck the living daylights out of them even though he was quite a femmy guy.

During one of our heart-to-heart chats over herbal tea (between clients), he started to tell me how much he wanted to be HIV positive. I thought he was crazy, but since then I've learned he's not alone; there are loads of other queers like him. He said he thought his life didn't have very much meaning, but if he became HIV positive that might change. After all, he was a therapist, and he'd be able to help people better if he knew their pain. He also said he couldn't stand the constant testing, the waiting, and the wondering. He said he sometimes had unsafe sex in the past, and he was sure he'd get HIV eventually. And sometimes, he said, he just wanted some big guy to give it to him.

"I know I sound crazy when I say that. . . ." He peered up at me with big blue Scottish eyes plunked in the centre of a bulldog face.

Well, I have to say I thought I was the right big guy to do it.

Our sex was great because Nick was one of those tops who just loves being topped. He loved it that my dick was bigger than his, that I weighed even more than him and could pin him down. To some, the whole thing might have looked like rape. At one point, for instance, it seemed like a porn story you might find on one of those barebacking Internet websites, except now and then he had to add a therapeutic phrase.

"Oh, you big loving man, are you going to fuck me? I'm scared! Are you going to fuck me with your HIV-positive dick?"

I played along. It was very sexy. "Yeah, I'm going to spill my infected seed in your ass, you big loving man."

Afterward, he cried like a baby. It was very edifying.

And from that day on, Nick has been a born-again HIV-infected messiah. He's told *everyone* he's positive.

"Being positive has changed my life," he says, and people are shocked, and he just smiles that horrible smile.

But it's true. He loves his trips to the doctor and his stultifying pill regimen. He loves shitting all the time and being nauseous, and he endures the humps that have started forming on his back. He tells everybody about his symptoms and is so cheery and "born again" that people are blown away. But unlike Whiny Betty, he doesn't do it to get sympathy from his family. For Nick, I think, it's something weirder. I don't think he really felt like an adult, experienced homosexual with wisdom and wit and whatever until he became HIV positive. It's like a membership card to an exclusive club.

Oh yeah, here's an AIDS joke for you.

Q: "What does AIDS stand for?"

A: "Anally inserted death sentence."

I always think of that joke when I think of Nick. It's an extra kick to know you're killing someone while making him very happy at the same time.

Second Prison Letter from
Cindy Lou Williams

Dear Mr. Klotz,

It was very informative to get your letter. I have to say right off that I am not yet comfortable calling you by your first name. I don't wish to be rude, but after all you are a killer — or at least an accused killer.

Truth be told — and we must always tell the truth, I think that it is very much the key to human relationships — I was offended by some of your language. I am a single woman in a small town. I still live with my mother. And though I was a child in the late 1960s, I'm afraid that the "sexual revolution" rather left me behind. Perhaps that's not a bad thing!

I have never understood the need to use off-colour language. I counted the number of times you used the "s-word" (ten) and the "f-word" (an unbelievable twenty-three times!). I substitute teach in the Wyoming school system, and my specialty is English. Thus, I count myself familiar with the language. I scrutinized your letter carefully, and, though it pained me to read those words over and over again, I have to say that I could find no logical reason for using so many expletives. For instance, at one point you talk about the "f-ing" judge and his "stupid" expression. As a cultured artist, you must be aware that words like "f-ing" and "stupid" are vague and overused. Think of how much more precise your description might be if you dispensed with the profanity and, instead, scoured your lexicon for the perfect descriptive word. Do they let you have dictionaries in there? If they do, I will get you one! Instead, and I know that I'm sounding very much like the elementary schoolteacher here, you might consider — rather than calling the judge "stupid" — you might describe his expression as "impenetrable." Alternatively, perhaps, you might speak of his "impervious gaze." How specific those expressions would be, and how they would lead us to picture the great judge sitting before us! A man who, I agree, *is* a formidable character.

I truly regret having to sound teacherly. As you are obviously a human being in need of help, I will read your letters no matter how much profanity you fill them with. I promise.

There is one other thing which offended me. I find it absolutely impossible to countenance your suggestion that Abraham Lincoln was, perhaps, a homosexual.

Where did you ever get such an idea?

Our beloved "honest Abe" was, I'm sure you're aware, one of the fathers of our country. Do I need to tell you that his name would most certainly fall into disrepute if it was to be learned that he was of that persuasion?

I also find it very difficult to imagine that he would have a lover named "Speed." How could that be? Isn't "speed" a modern term or a slang name for an illegal drug? I cannot possibly picture this fine statesman as you describe him. "Rolling around in bed and planting passionate kisses on his young lover"!!!

Again, your letters can do without these graphic descriptions and extreme suggestions. You are a passionate scribe with a great deal to say. I will always listen.

You know, sometimes I think that you put all those shocking things into your letter just to put me off! Well, I won't be put off. I am not completely out of touch, you know!

Now, it has come to my attention that you yourself are an acknowledged homosexual. Is this true? Don't worry, if it's a secret, I won't tell anyone.

I will admit that, due to my upbringing, I'm not very informed about homosexuals. We have no homosexuals in Wyoming. Perhaps there *are* one or two, but they seem to keep to themselves!

My father, may he rest in peace, was seriously opposed to homosexuality. He was a member of a very interesting organization, Save Our Children from Homosexuals Incorporated. Later they were called The Anita Bryant Ministries. He had her books and pamphlets around the house, and they inevitably influenced my opinions. Anita used to talk about how single men engage in criminal activity more than married ones. I can't help wondering if there is some connection between your own unmarried status and the charges against you. There is something about that holy union which softens a man, which makes him more gentle and caring. Whatever you say, I don't think you can deny the positive influence of a woman on a man's life! Although I'm past my prime, I'm still a woman, and I think that I have something to offer to the right man.

Anita Bryant also mentioned another interesting fact in her book. I will speak graphically here, but it is in the service of frankness and clarity. She often spoke of the fact that homosexuals "eat" sperm. When I was a child, I didn't know what this meant. Now that I am older and wiser in the ways of the world, I understand. And she wisely observed that to eat sperm is to eat human life. Certainly there is some truth in this. Certainly it is not right to eat human life. If everyone did, how would our species survive?

Anyway, I'm hoping that you can clean up your letters a little so that they will be easier for me to read. But, rest assured, any letter that you send will get a reply. I want you to know that you're not alone in there. That, no matter what, someone has hope for your immortal soul.

That's me.

Anyway, keep a stiff upper lip and write back.

Sincerely,

Cindy Lou Williams

What Is Evil?

Well, I am. I certainly am. And proud of it. If you're bored or something, then just break a few taboos. You'll feel a lot better.

Of course, I could point to a lot of examples in the animal kingdom that would convince you evil is just a part of life. Yes, lions eat pretty little deer, just as hawks eat pretty little rabbits.

The important thing to remember is you can't fight evil. It's just there. It's best to just give in. Even to want it. Enjoy death. Yearn for sickness. That's one way of dealing with the whole evil thing.

Sorry. That isn't my theme here. (Remember to stick to the "theme.")

I just thought you might be interested in a demented killer's view of this stupid world. We can learn something from all points of view, can't we? Hey, aren't you a liberal?

So here are three examples of what I consider to be evil things or persons or acts or . . . whatever.

1. GLENN CLOSE

Don't get me wrong. I think she's a fabulous actress and everything. Really. And it's been tough for her not being pretty in any traditional way. It's not her fault she always plays evil characters. After all, she's been typecast because she's not perfectly beautiful.

But I draw the line at *Fatal Attraction.*

Not that I don't like the movie. I love it. Who wouldn't? It's fabulously suspenseful, and everyone is very good. And, oh, when she kills the bunny. When she boils it! That's one of my favourite parts.

But how, you tell me how, *could* Glenn Close star in that movie? I mean, hasn't *Fatal Attraction* set women's lib back a hundred years? We finally get a strong and sexual woman in a film, and what is she? A clingy killer. I mean, this woman is far worse than I am. She doesn't kill the nerd because she wants to see him dead; she kills him because she's weak and loves him so much. Because her feelings have been hurt. Hey, ain't that just like a woman?

Can you explain something to me? How could any self-respecting woman have had anything to do with the making of that movie? She'd have had to value money and fame over ideas. Because no recent movie has done more to help reinforce female stereotypes. Thank you, Glenn Close, for helping us all to see women as vile clingy cunts with teeth.

Making that movie was evil, Glenn. You are evil.

2. MY FRIEND NIGEL'S BOYFRIEND, SAM

I know this very good-looking guy. Nigel is a tall journalist type with parents who were both teachers — he had a very cultured upbringing. We used to drink and get stoned together. Until he decided to fall in love with this stupid creep named Sam.

Sam is a short redheaded eternally boyish-looking guy with freckles. He looked twelve even though he was almost twenty-five. Because Nigel was madly in love with him, he didn't have time for me anymore. Welcome to the gay lifestyle! Now and then, he'd feel guilty because I was single (sometimes it's hard for us killers to get a date!), and he'd invite me over to dinner. These dinners were tawdry affairs. At some point during the evening, usually while Nigel was busy cooking (his mother, besides being an English teacher, was a dynamite cook), beguiling Sam would corner me over a glass of wine and start confessing his sexual frustrations.

"How's it going?" I'd ask, just trying to be friendly.

"All right," Sam would say, sounding pretty undecided.

"What's wrong?"

"Well, I don't know if I should talk about it," he'd say.

"Well, if you don't want to talk about it, then don't."

"But I *do*," he'd say.

"Well, what, then?" I'd already be annoyed.

"Well, Nigel and I are having some problems."

And I'd continue to listen. Not because I'm an asshole but because — even though I'm a killer — I'm somehow always in a state of disbelief about how evil people can be sometimes. Evil in subtle ways.

"The thing is Nigel and I are having some . . . sexual problems."

"Oh yeah?" I'd say, sort of wondering why Nigel hadn't told me. After all, before he started living with this creep, we talked about everything.

"I don't know. I just don't think monogamy is for me. I'm just always so . . . tempted." Then he'd move closer to me and take a sip out of his drink, peering over the rim of the glass with those little-boy eyes. I'm not kidding.

At the time, I was so innocent about the sexual crap that goes on in this world I didn't realize he was coming on to me. I just couldn't imagine that my best friend's lover would try to get me into bed. I mean, some things are worse than murder. Personally, I'd rather kill one of my best friends than try to get his lover into bed. This is a *friend* we're talking about. That's just *not nice*.

So Sam went on to have several affairs. I actually witnessed one. Sam used to work all day loading boxes. I happened to take a walk behind his company one day — I like to hang out in alleys — and he was boffing this burly worker in a dark corner in broad daylight! I'd find out about Sam's sleazy indiscretions way before Nigel did, and I could never tell Nigel, and it was just so . . . ugh.

Anyway, finally, the eternally boyish Sam told Nigel he was "an ugly old fag." Can you believe it? Can you believe he said that to his lover? So Nigel broke up with him. But when Sam came crawling back, Nigel started up with him again. Can you imagine that? Accepting a lover back into your arms after he says you're "an ugly old fag"? I can't.

Of course, I had to be nice about it and go to their dinners as if nothing had happened. Sam would still drag me into a corner after the first glass of wine and say, "Can we talk?"

I'd just say, "No."

Believe it or not, they're still together. They'll probably be together forever. I guess it's what they call true love. Except every day Nigel ages a little more and thinks about Sam's comment. I know he does. And Nigel has become *so old* (he's skinny and has such dry skin he tends to get wrinkles) he's paranoid about wanting to break up. He's afraid he'll never meet another "Mister Right," another young freckled muscleboy, at his advanced age. I mean, he must be at least thirty-three, for Christ's sake.

I think the way Sam treats Nigel is evil.

3. THE AUDIENCE FOR *CHERIE*

A couple of years ago, a friend of mine wrote a wonderful play based on the Colette novel *Cherie*. Okay, the play wasn't perfect. But it was nearly perfect. I don't know if you know the novel — it's about this old whore who falls in love with a boy. Very gay. She has an affair with the kid. And then they break up, and the boy tries to come back. But she won't let him. She's grown older and accepted that it's over. But the boy hasn't. He's a callow youth who doesn't know how to deal with the world because he's always been a gigolo. So he shoots himself.

What a great plot, huh?

Well, everything was right about that production. The woman playing the whore had big tits and wasn't afraid to show them. The boy playing the boy was very talented and had a lithe but very hard muscular body — which he showed off every other second, willingly, without fear. The set was beautiful: these lovely curtains that were sort of see-through and draped over everything. I loved it. And the lighting was great too. The designers created colours that I'd never seen.

But the strangest thing happened.

Actually, it wasn't strange at all.

The play was performed in a church hall. Who knows why? It was a small, semiprofessional production. Many of the people who came to see the show were older and religious. And, you know, pinched. Pinched old faces and crusty old bodies that had been washed over and over with soap until they were dry and rough and red. These people had never known pleasure.

And the audience was filled, especially, with old women. Women who'd never known pleasure.

Every night they watched this beautiful, sad story about a woman whose life was totally devoted to pleasure. And every night they sat there in stunned silence.

They didn't laugh when the play was funny. They didn't clap at the intermission. Occasionally, one of the shocked crusty matrons would place a hand over a tight little mouth opened to form a tiny O, and a breathless gasp of disgust would escape from her guts, along with the stench of repression.

The young actor playing Cherie, the boy, was brilliant and sensitive. The lack of audience response hurt him deeply. Being a good but inexperienced actor, he was so immersed in the part he could no longer separate the hurt Cherie felt from his own pain. He became an open wound.

And then one night, near the end of the play, came the unfortunate line. "How long will this go on?" said the innocent, staring at the audience balefully.

And one of the dried-up old prunes in the audience giggled. It was a vile, bitter, contemptuous sound. It was the giggle of a vagina that had never been moist, of breasts that had never been jiggled or kissed.

The interruption so shocked the boy he almost couldn't continue. But he did. After all, he was a professional.

Later, when the play was over and the rest of the cast had gone, the stage manager left the boy alone in the theatre. The pale hard boy picked up the starter pistol and aimed it at his head at close range and killed himself.

The police called it suicide.

I call it murder.

The audience killed that boy. That audience was evil.

My Neighbours

Why am I going to tell you another story about my neighbours?

I'm afraid that you might not think I'm really evil. You may well have thought, "Oh, he's just killing silly homosexuals. Silly drag queens — the lowest of the low, the scum of the earth. Nick and Whiny Betty, the world's the same with or without them. They are inconsequential. Why doesn't he kill someone of consequence?"

But I have. I want you to know I have.

Third Prison Letter from Cindy Lou Williams

Dear Mr. Klotz,

Goodness. When are they going to start your trial? I know that proceedings often get mired in red tape, but this is ridiculous. I am in a state of pitiful suspense. I long to hear you speak! I just know that you will have a kind and cultured voice, whatever atrocities you have committed.

Seeing you there at the defence desk, waiting for the endless formalities to end, I can tell that you are a patient person at least.

As per your request, well, I almost feel silly describing myself to you. You want to know what I look like, but. . . . Can't you tell who I am? I suppose that it's stupid of me to think that you would know. I'll give you a hint. I always wear a flowered dress — I have a weakness for flowers. There is a gold kitten pin attached to the left upper side of my dress, my good-luck charm. My hair is dark brown and limper and flatter than it should be. I have it in a sort of pixie cut, it's more flattering to my rounded face; at least that's what everyone says.

Your boredom has led you to ask me for a story, so I will certainly oblige. I enjoy talking about my life. I suppose that most people who've had uneventful lives feel that way. You, on the other hand, have lived intensely, I just know it. You must tell me more about your life in your next letter. I am very interested. And I can handle it all, I know that I can, bad words and all.

So, the story of the June Bug Epidemic. Perhaps the first thing that I should say about it is that it didn't have anything at all to do with June bugs, strange as that may seem. That is, it did have to do with bugs. Or, rather, mites. I think. Oh dear, I'd better start at the beginning. The important thing to remember is that June bug in this case does not refer to those giant, scary bugs — I hate them — that people call June bugs. But rather to an insect infestation which occurred in June. Hence the name.

To begin at the beginning, my mother, Hester, used to work at Wyoming Mills, a clothing plant located in our town (it's still there). It's one of the few businesses in our town which has nothing to do with oil, or the oil industry, besides the Mace factory. After all, you can't make dresses out of oil — or at least they wouldn't be very pretty!

At the time, my father was on disability from Standard Oil. He had fallen on a slippery patch and hurt his back — which is why he had enough time to read all about Anita Bryant and her ministries. So our only money — besides his disability money, which went to his treatments — came from my mother's job at Wyoming Mills.

My mother didn't like what she did very much. She enjoyed the fact that there were so many other ladies there — it was mostly women there, in the actual dressmaking department. But she didn't like cutting dress patterns. It was real drudgery, and it hurt her hands. Her hands are my mother's most beautiful feature. When she was young, a real professional photographer took photos of her hands. They're very pretty. She could have been a hand model. At Wyoming Mills, her hands were always getting red and sometimes cut.

And in June, which was the month of the epidemic, things got very pressured. The personnel director, Hiram P. Grant, was a real pig. I don't use that word lightly. He actually looked like one! He was a very oppressive boss. Nothing meant more to him than productivity — I always thought it might be his middle name! Mr. Grant used to inspect the plant every day, if you can imagine. He would march up and down the aisles and make a big stink if some woman wasn't working fast enough. My mother told me that one day he made a spectacle of her in front of the other employees. He yelled at her for working too slowly. This was at a time when her hands were bleeding from accidents with the scissors. Of course, it was incredibly hot that June, and because of the fall deadline — the dresses were needed for the fall fashion houses — the pressure was unbearable.

So, what should happen in the middle of all this? The June Bug Epidemic. For weeks, my mother had been coming home complaining of a rash (this was late May). She went to the doctor, and he said, "Oh, it's just a heat rash, don't worry about it." But my mother didn't think that it was a rash because the marks spread too far over her body. Never one to swim with the tide, when my mother has a thought, she speaks it, it's often gotten her into trouble, and it's made her into quite a handful in her old age.

So, one day my mother found a tiny bug in her underpants. It was very gross. We looked at it under a microscope, and it looked something like a flea. So we looked up fleas in the encyclopedia. But it wasn't a flea. Just . . . similar.

Later (it was a fine, hot Wednesday in June) my mother went

to work. At school, an announcement came over the loudspeaker. There were never announcements unless there was a fire drill, so we were all pretty surprised. The principal said that there was some sort of epidemic at the plant. Now, a lot of the students' mothers worked at the plant, so they decided to close the school for the day. I was very frightened. I'll never forget that walk home. In fact, it was more like a run. I remember thinking, "What a pretty day! How much nicer it would be to be playing." I was a very discombobulated young lady, to say the least!

When I got home, my mother was lying on the sofa. My father was marching around yelling about Hiram. "That Hiram P. Grant has got some nerve!" And then he yelled at my mother — which didn't help matters. "Did you report this?" he asked.

And my mother, crying, said, "Yes, of course, weeks ago, Fred. Weeks ago!"

"I can't believe he let it get this bad. Look at you! What did the doctor say?"

"He said for me to get a rest."

"Well, are you?"

"Not with you marching around and yelling!"

They went on like that.

My mother looked horrible. There were bites all over her body — as far as I could see — and she was red in the face. "I feel as if my head is going to burst!" she said.

"Where's the doctor! Get the doctor!" my father yelled.

I was about to run out the door.

My mother started sobbing. "It's no use . . . it's no use . . . he examined me from head to toe." Then, all of a sudden, she screamed, "Oh, my God! My foot is numb! My foot is numb! What's happening to me? God help me! I can't feel anything in my foot!"

She was hysterical. It's horrible to see your mother like that. For me, it was a turning point. It may well have been my entry into adulthood.

My father yelled at me, "Will you go and get the frigging doctor!"

I was really scared. My father never actually swore before, even when he was really mad. Not like you, Mr. Klotz. Of course, he's never spent any time in New York City. Perhaps that's the reason. Anyway, I ran out the door.

I should say that I didn't go directly to the doctor. I stopped along the way, at The Fountainhead monument. Perhaps I should explain. In the centre of our town, in front of the new town hall, is a statue dedicated to Ayn Rand's novel. It's called The Fountainhead, and it's very futuristic. I've always been an admirer of Miss Rand's work, and I've found the statue to be an inspiration in times of stress. So, I admit that I dawdled on the way to the doctor, but I was very conflicted, what with my mother crying and my father swearing. The statue, as usual, helped me to collect my thoughts, and I got the doctor and dragged him back to —

I'm sorry, I'll have to stop here. My mother is calling me. What an irony. She seems to be having one of her bad spells — just when I'm telling you about them! But I know that you really need an entertaining story, so I'll post this.

Keep up your spirits. Your letters are so short that I don't really feel that I know you yet. Someday maybe we could meet? Or is that permitted? Anyway, I have to sign off. Chin up.

Your friend indeed,
Cindy Lou Williams

My Damned Fucking Stupid Neighbours

Just so you don't think I kill only silly suicidal people, I want to tell you about my other neighbours. They're people who are a lot harder to kill. People who are really worth killing. Interesting, passionate people. People with real human potential. People who, when *they* die, are a loss to the human race.

But first I want to tell you about The Crown Prince. He lives down the hall. He's not relevant, really. Except his craziness sure tells you something about the human capacity for delusion. The weird thing about him is he's not HIV positive. He makes sure to tell you that. It's one of the reasons why he always has his nose in the air. He belongs to the aristocracy of fags that has the approval of the medical establishment. They're "clean" somehow. God knows how. Of course, that doesn't do much to modify his ugliness and the fact that he lives in a fantasy world of his own design.

Anyway, he's about forty-five years old, though he looks much older, and has a small smart beard and longish hair. He thinks he looks distinguished, and he claims to be descended from the crown heads of Europe. Specifically — you guessed it — Czar Nicholas II. He claims to have all sorts of proof, but I've never actually seen any. His apartment is certainly filled with godawful real antiques — not fake junk as in Whiny Betty's place. Of course, he wants me to plug his ass because he likes big scary guys like me. But I wouldn't even give him AIDS. That's how contemptuous I am of him.

My favourite story about The Crown Prince relates to a Christmas card he sent to me a couple of years ago. Enclosed with it was a letter. It was written in this sort of cramped, grand script that you might associate with a rich European grandmother. It read:

Dear Kasper,

I would like to take this opportunity to offer you many thanks for the kind Christmas epistle that I received from you.

I want to make it very clear that such old-fashioned gestures truly mean something. They remind me of another era — a grander, more eliquent [sic] era where not only the aristocacy [sic] had "manners."

Yours truly,
    Karl Rantinovich Esq.

The saddest thing about this letter, of course, is that I never sent him a fucking epistle in my life. I never even sent him a Christmas card. So the letter he was supposedly responding to existed only in his demented imagination. On top of that, there's his feigned knowledge of a "grander" era. We're supposed to believe this ugly lonely old fag down the hall used to dine with kings? Right. I mean, how do you explain his spelling? As far as I know, Russian aristocrats were hemophiliacs, not dyslexics.

It's interesting to note, if you're into "noting" things, that Karl's particular delusion is more widespread than most people are probably aware. That is, many people, when they go nuts, think they are the lost descendants of White Russians. I don't know if it's the success of that *Anastasia* movie, with Ingrid Bergman, the one they made in the 1960s, or what. But next to being carried away by aliens and anally probed, being a descendant of Czar Nicholas II is apparently the most popular psych fantasy.

So if you're considering going nuts, just remember every one of the Romanovs, including cute little Anastasia, was gunned to death in a cellar. They finally found all the DNA samples they needed to prove it. So just lay off, will ya?

Okay, I've wasted enough time on my incredibly delusional neighbour. Now it's time to tell you about my second biggest achievement as a natural-born killer: Alphonse.

Unlike Whiny Betty or Nick, Alphonse is a pretty nice guy. Very nice, actually. That's why we were lovers.

Yeah, I have a love life. Jeez. Killers fall in love too. And they don't always kill their boyfriends. Or girlfriends. Of course, when it came to Alphonse, I couldn't resist giving him AIDS.

Alphonse was kind of a perfect person. When I met him, he was seeing this great therapist, Anna. She was really cool. I met her at a party once. Yes, ugly smelly killers go to parties too. She was something called a "narrative" therapist. Which means she helps you to tell your "story."

Alphonse's story was that he was gifted but wasn't sure how. His parents were both professors, and he came from an intellectually privileged, hippie-esque environment. His folks were almost the most intelligent, perfect people who ever lived. When they found out he was gay, they were basically, well, pleased.

Alphonse never wanted for stimulation or understanding. Of course, he did have to deal with a world that is pretty stupid and hateful, but don't we all? Try getting sympathy for that one.

Anyway, having parents who were so fucking smart and open-minded meant Alphonse always felt obligated to "be" something great and creative. Only he could never figure out what his little niche was.

He was also a handsome slender young guy with an enormous cock, by the way. Just my type.

Anna, the narrative therapist, helped Alphonse a lot. She made him realize there were many oppressive "stories" out there in the culture. Stories that said he "should" do this or that with his life because he was male, or gay, or gifted, or whatever. So, not being obligated to follow any particular "story," Alphonse sort of popped around and tried everything. And he was pretty good at everything. He used to take photographs, for instance. Photographs of sculptures, mainly nude men, and of fabrics. He had some great close-ups of leopard skin. And sometimes he acted in plays. He wasn't a great actor. But nobody seemed to mind. He was kind and gay and elegant.

I think what turned Alphonse on to me was the fact I'm an artist. I think he'd had a lot of dumb boyfriends and finally come to the point where someone ugly and smelly like me would be okay, because at least I could entertain him. And we did have fun for a while. Alphonse didn't have any trouble being monogamous. He wasn't too aware of sex, and he wasn't too interested in it. But he'd let me suck his big dick now and then, which was enough for me. So I never told him I was a slut from hell. I guess he figured that, because I'm so unattractive, no one would ever want to fuck me.

Nothing could be further from the truth.

I didn't think I'd have to kill him, I really didn't. Then a weird thing happened. Alphonse got really stupid about the whole idea of "safe sex." So I decided I'd have to kill him.

I don't know if you're aware of the whole history of safe sex. Here's a crash course. When they announced the big news in 1984, or whenever it was, that AIDS is caused by HIV, all the right-wing evangelist types thought it meant the end of homosexuality. They thought God was finally exacting retribution on homosexuals for all their perverted acts.

Oh, yeah. Here's an AIDS joke for you.

Q: What do you call homosexuals camping out at the North Pole?

A: KoolAIDS.

How about another brilliant variation on the same theme?

Q: What do you call homosexuals on roller skates?

A: RolAIDS.

So, to combat these hateful beliefs, all the gay leaders came to the same conclusion: everyone would use condoms. The whole idea of safe sex is that you can have as much fun as you used to — "Maybe even more!" the cheery safe sex ads say — if you just use condoms. Look how much fun condoms are! They tell you how much fun it is to blow condoms up like balloons. Right. What a turn on. And then there are all the S/M freaks who piss into condoms while they're wearing them. Then they break the condoms and let the piss spill all over. Hey, that sounds like great fun too.

If you're fucking nuts.

No, truth be told, condoms are a pain. Nobody likes them. Especially not guys who really enjoy getting fucked up the ass. They hate them. The whole point of getting fucked is that you get that feeling of skin on flesh, of the dick rubbing against the inside of the asshole. (I hope you didn't just eat lunch or something.) The only people who use condoms these days are fags. Straight people don't use them (come on, be honest!) because the horrible truth nobody will speak is this: straight people don't get AIDS from sex. I ought to know, I've given it to enough people. And they were all fags. Fags who were stupid in some way.

So, even though there's been this big safe sex campaign — so fags can still be fags — a lot of fags hate safe sex and will have nothing to do with it. Guys like Nick, who sure enjoyed receiving my positive come up his big hairy butt. And then there are all the fags who'd never come out against condoms, because they're too nice and intelligent, but who still miss the old sensation. Now, Alphonse was one of those guys. Even though he had a big dick, he just loved to get fucked by mine. So I'd oblige him, always using a condom, of course, because intelligent fags always use condoms, right? Then one day Alphonse started to talk about "negotiated safety."

"What's that?" I asked.

"Oh, it's this new idea they've come up with in Australia."

"Hey, I thought they didn't have any homosexuals in Australia." I was trying to be humorous. See? Even killers can be funny.

And he said, "Yeah, right, well, in Australia they're trying this thing where couples can negotiate doing away with condoms."

"Oh yeah, how do they do that?" I didn't really give a fuck. I love fucking people with or without condoms, and frankly it doesn't make any difference to me. My dick is so big I always get friction unless the guy is the Carlsbad Caverns or something.

"Well, this is how it works. Sit down, and we can read this together."

Alphonse always loved the idea of us reading things together and working stuff out. It was very corny.

Anyway, this pamphlet he had was filled with totally crazy garbage. Worse, Alphonse bought it. He's sure regretting it now, downstairs.

The idea behind "negotiated safety" is that, if you and your "partner" — I hate that word, what are we, a fucking skating routine or something? — have enough love and trust and all that other gunky shit, you're allowed to dispense with safe sex, gradually and carefully. How do you do that? By

(a) having long talks
(b) being honest
(c) getting tested for HIV all the time
(d) promising not to fuck anybody else
(e) trusting each other
(f) deciding to stop using condoms together.

Have you got it? If two people love each other and trust each other enough, if they're in a committed, long-term, monogamous relationship, and if they test negative for HIV over and over again, then they can quit having safe sex. AIDS organizations all over the world now condone this shit.

I couldn't believe it. I was amazed. It pissed me off that Alphonse would fall for it, so I decided I had to kill him.

I know that sounds harsh, but after all I'm a killer. I'm damn proud of it, actually. And Alphonse was being so stupid.

Sure, you might say, "Is that any reason to kill him?"

"For a killer, yes."

You might also say, "But didn't you love Alphonse?"

"Yes. Until he suggested this stupid idea."

Can I tell you something else? It's worse when smart people are stupid than when stupid people are stupid. I mean, Nick and Whiny Betty were idiots from the moment I met them, so it was easy to decide to do away with them. But Alphonse was different. He had potential, the real possibility of being an interesting human being. But he fucked it up. Big time. As soon as he suggested this shit, it became clear that Alphonse, even though he was talented and gifted and intelligent, was just as dumb as all the other silly fags. I hated him for it. And wanted to kill him. So I infected him. It was easy, actually. Not stressful at all. Kinda fun.

I just lied to him.

Lying has never been a problem for me. He asked me if I was HIV positive, and I said no. Then he asked me if I'd ever been unfaithful to him, and I said no. I knew he'd feel guilty about asking me to get an AIDS test — so there was no problem with that. We just "trusted" and "loved" each other.

Then we had a candlelit bathtub fuck — without a condom. We used baby oil, which is great because it doesn't dissolve in water, plus it destroys condoms; you can't even use it with condoms. We both had fabulous orgasms.

Now Alphonse is sick. As a dog. Almost dead. Because he loved me. Because he loved and trusted me.

Too fucking bad.

Now and then, Alphonse — who is skinny and hollow-eyed and wracked with pneumonia — will bang on my floor with a broom handle. I'll go out and buy him some ginger ale and crackers. He can't hold anything much down, but I don't feel bad at all. I look at him and think, "That stupid fucker deserved it."

Maybe I'll tell him before he dies. He doesn't suspect me yet. You know, he believes in love and trust and honesty and all that shit. Maybe on his deathbed I'll tell him. "Hey, I did this to you." Then maybe he'll be sorry for having been so fucking stupid.

Stupidity is one thing I just can't stand, ya know?

Fourth Prison Letter from
Cindy Lou Williams

Dear Mr. Klotz,

Well, I have to say that I'm perturbed. I've never been one to keep her feelings to herself.

Your last letter was upsetting, I have to say. Let's start at the beginning. In your letter before that, you asked me how I look. In my swift and good-natured letter of reply, I gave you what I thought was an accurate description of my outward, physical self. I offered the description to a friend of mine, and she agreed that it was, indeed, accurate. The description was certainly not meant to be flirtatious in any way.

What do you offer me in reply? An insult to my dignity. You suggest that I "sound," to use your own words "very f—-able." (I'm afraid that I am not capable of writing the f-word, nor do I think it necessary to do so in this context!)

I have to say that, in addition to being angry, I am quite confused. My understanding is that you are a person who has chosen the homosexual lifestyle. Homosexual persons, I believe, are generally attracted to those of the same sex, sexually. Therefore, how in heaven's name would you even know whether or not I was, in fact, "f—-able?" Not that I consider being "f—-able" a desirable thing. I most certainly do not. Really, Mr. Klotz. I am trying to help you. I don't see what possible good it can do you to alienate me. I'm sure that I am one of your only friends. They tell me, at any rate, that you have no visitors.

The second thing that I would like to confront you about is your criticism of Miss Ayn Rand. Not that I find it surprising. Reaction to her work is mixed. She is a controversial and challenging author. But I have always contended that it is irresponsible to throw about the word *fascist*. I do not think that she is a "fascist" writer. I do not even think that a writer can be "fascist." Except, perhaps, Emmanuel Kant. Miss Rand's essays explore the fascist aspects of this particular philosopher.

Now, I'm not a student of economics, but I do not believe Ayn Rand theorizes that "the rich should eat the poor." You may have meant it as an unkind exaggeration. She believes that the rich should be rewarded for their efforts and that the work of the rich, and their brilliance, ultimately benefit the poor. I have to say that I have certainly observed these facts to be true — at least in my humble estimation — in my little hometown. The corporation of Standard Oil has greatly benefited our modest burgh.

No, my attraction to the works of Ayn Rand is neither economic nor political. It is personal and, well, romantic. By romantic, I mean her vision of man and her passion for the heroic. In *The Fountainhead*, her leading character, Howard Roark, is a vision of man as he was meant to be. The way that Dominique Francon feels about him seems right to me. She surrenders herself because he is her "highest value." That is always the way I have imagined love to be, and I have never lowered my standards. It's caused me many a lonely night!

Now that we've done away with all that, I want to assure you that, once I've aired a grievance, I never hold a grudge. I'm sure that you will apologize for treating me, if I may put it bluntly, like a tart. And since you seemed to be interested in the June bug story, I'll continue relating it to you.

When we last left my mother, she had fainted from the pain and worrying that her head "would burst." I ran to get the doctor — no easy feat because he was visiting other patients who were also stricken and bedridden. When the doctor arrived, it was very strange. Even though my mother was obviously in pain, he refused to find anything wrong with her. Most of his conclusions were based on the fact that she didn't have a temperature. This was the oddest thing. I mean, my mother was obviously tortured, anyone could see that — her face was red, and she was rolling around on the couch and holding her calf. She couldn't move her leg without experiencing excruciating cramps!

My father even asked, "Are you accusing my wife of faking this illness?"

The doctor said that he wasn't and that, indeed, this was the tenth patient he'd seen with *exactly the same symptoms.*

Exactly the same.

The head almost bursting, the red face, the fainting, the pain in the calves, and the bites. I told him that I thought surely it was a bite. I ran and got Mother's underpants and showed him the tiny bug.

He said, "It looks like a mite!" and put it into a plastic bag.

Then he gave my mother a pill to calm her and a shot to ease the pain, and then he left. She slept soundly after that all night and into the next day.

When I went to school in the morning, I discovered that many of the other children had mothers who'd also been stricken. The plant was closed the next day, and then it was Sunday, when, of course, no one went to work. Meanwhile, my mother got better, though she was afraid of going back to work. Afraid that another bug would get her. On Monday morning, we called and discovered that the plant was open. Mr. Hiram P. Grant's secretary told us that the epidemic was over. He said that the plant had been sprayed by the exterminator, and there were no more bugs to hurt any of the women.

My mother and the other women went to work, and it was never spoken of again.

With everything back to normal, no one talked about the epidemic. And no one seemed to suffer permanent side effects. These days my mother suffers from arthritis, and it causes her a lot of pain. But it has nothing to do with that bug in June.

That should be the end of the story. Except that it isn't.

Years later I was assigned a project for health class. This was a time before health classes everywhere became obsessed with you know what. The project was about "Great Epidemics of History." I got it into my head to write about the June Bug Epidemic, but doing the research was difficult. I went to our family doctor, and he said, "There was no epidemic. Your mother was just sick."

I didn't know what he was talking about. After all, I was there. I saw it. I went to school and talked to all the other kids who had sick mothers.

"No," he said, "there was no *epidemic*. A lot of people just happened to get sick at the same time, that's all. Why don't you consider researching Typhoid Mary? Typhoid, now there's a fascinating epidemic!"

Well, I had considered Typhoid Mary, but I didn't want to do my project on her. Typhoid was a very popular epidemic project. Two other students — girls I was *really* competitive with at the time — were already doing her. Besides, everybody knows the story of Typhoid Mary.

I wanted to do something else. I decided to ask the school nurse, who was a very interesting lady. I always liked her, but I didn't know why. She was "different." A new person around town, she had worked in a big city — Indianapolis — before settling in our environs. Her name was Miss Kramm. She was large and wore her hair very short. Like me these days, I assume she had decided that a short cut would be more flattering to her face. I was pretty impressed with her. She was kind of a romantic figure for me, being from the big city. So I interviewed Miss Kramm about the June Bug Epidemic. What she told me was very strange.

"There was no epidemic," she said, and at first I thought she was echoing the words of our family doctor. But she wasn't. "It was a case of mass hysteria."

"Mass hysteria?" I didn't know what that was.

"Well," she said, "mass hysteria is a condition where people's minds create an illness in their bodies."

"Are you saying that my mother wasn't really sick? I saw her."

"Not at all," said Miss Kramm, "I'm sure she was very ill. People can even die from hysteria. You see, sometimes when people believe they are ill it is just as good as being ill. I've read about the June Bug Case. It's very famous."

"It is?" I said. I was surprised that our town was famous for anything.

"Oh, yes," she said, "it's written up in all the journals of psycho-history."

I wanted to learn more about psychohistory, so I went to the library and looked it up. Sure enough, it's a science, and believe it or not there were books that had lots of stuff about my home-town. My own little town, written up in the medical journals! And they had another epidemic of "mass hysteria" in Kyoto, Japan. And I read all about The Phantom Anesthetist of Altoona. It was fascinating.

Oh my, I've gone on and on. It's time for me to stop.

In signing off, let me reiterate that I was deeply hurt by your implication. I am not, and never have been, a tart. Quite the oppo-site is true. However, the fact that you have treated me in this way leads me to treat you in another way. Henceforth, I will consider you a confused person rather than a homosexual.

Don't get depressed.

Yours,

Cindy Lou Williams

Why You Are Deluded

You are deluded because you think you are safe. You think you are a nice person. You think heterosexuals don't get "it." I lied. They do. See how tricky I can be?

You are deluded because you have created a lovely life for yourself, one in which there is no mouth cancer.

Let me tell you the story of Mickey.

Mickey was a close friend of mine. No, I didn't kill him. I don't kill everybody! He lived in a big gay house with me, a house populated by gay men. One of my straight friends used to call it The AIDS Farm. But hey, none of us is dead from AIDS yet. How about that?

Mickey was this incredibly beautiful boy who was very active in the Communist Party. I didn't really understand his ideas. He'd graduated with a master's degree in Trotsky or something. Anyway, anytime he opened his beautiful mouth to talk about his theories, I'd just zone out. But it was very sexy, because boys as beautiful as Mickey usually don't have any ideas about anything.

Let me describe him. He had dark, dark brown eyes — almost black — and straight, straight lips. And a shock of straight black hair that fell down over his eyes — very cruelly. He was slender, and he was hard, everywhere. I never saw his dick, but I have no reason to believe it wasn't as beautiful as the rest of him.

I used to fantasize a lot about fucking Mickey. I never fantasized about giving him AIDS, though. He was too perfect. If I had ever managed to get him into bed, it might have happened. There was always a chance, killing people is just too much fun. But Mickey had no need to fuck big ugly guys like me. No, he had bigger fish to fry. Which meant every beautiful kid in town. I swear, every time a new one appeared, Mickey was, metaphorically, waiting at the bus depot for him. If we were out at a bar for the evening, I'd point to a new face, and Mickey would say, "Done him. Done him. Oh yeah, done *him*, wow."

Mickey had done everybody. He was so beautiful people would just throw themselves in front of him and ask to get fucked. It was very demoralizing for a lot of guys hanging out with Mickey.

Not me, though. Because I look a bit like Charles Laughton, I'm used to being ignored. When we went out together, it was kind of like Beauty and the Beast. Being with Mickey could make you feel anonymous — which is okay sometimes. It was like wearing a disguise, because no one looked at you, only at him.

We talked mainly about boys. And we never talked about AIDS. Actually, I don't think he thought about it much. Anyway, Mickey was so beautiful it seemed inappropriate to discuss AIDS when he was around. He'd never die of AIDS. I just knew it. Mickey was too beautiful to think about anything but communism and fucking. Fucking and communism. Fucking communism.

God, he was perfect.

Then one day he moved. Suddenly. It was really weird. Seems there were more communists in San Francisco, so he went there. I didn't hear about him much. Now and then, of course, people would go to visit San Francisco — which had been hit so hard by the "plague" that they were still counting the dead — and I'd ask them how Mickey was.

"Oh, fine," they'd say.

Of course he was "fine." Mickey would always be fine.

Finally news came that Mickey was sick. I assumed it was AIDS, of course. But my San Francisco sources said it was something else. Right. I never thought Mickey would get AIDS because he was so beautiful. But, you know, it *was* something else.

Mouth cancer. I can't imagine anything more horrific. He was very ill with it, and in trying to save his life they ended up cutting up his face. For a while, beautiful, perfect Mickey was walking around San Francisco missing half his nose and half his jaw. Lovely, perfect Mickey. It would have been a nightmare for anyone, but for a perfect boy? Even if you're a devoted communist, with lots of friends in the "party," it's pretty tragic to be missing your face.

Mickey died a couple of years later when there wasn't any more of his face to cut up.

Whenever I get too complacent about anything now, I just think about Mickey.

Just remember, you are deluded.

You're deluded because you think that you'll live for a long time and that your life is going to continue to be pleasant.

You won't. And it's not.

How You Will Recognize Me

So now that you know I look a bit like Quasimodo, you probably feel safe.

"Oh, I'd never sleep with Kasper! I'd never sleep with a fat, humpbacked, ugly, greasy guy like him. He's the AIDS guy! No, I'll never get AIDS."

But this is just what I look like today. I take many forms, I have many disguises.

When I was with Mickey, I was invisible. When I'm with certain men, I'm their deepest, darkest fantasy. They're the ones who like guys with bad teeth and ripped hats — but more about that later. For some men, I'm their every beautiful dream. If you want to know how you'll recognize me — sorry, you can't. I'm everywhere. I'm where you least expect me to be. And I'm where you'd rather not look. Turn around! You just missed me. I'm gone.

But I'll be back.

Conversation Overheard at the Local Gay Coffee Shop

"So what's the news?"

"Well. . . ."

"Don't torture me. Well what?"

"Well. . . ."

"You bitch — spill!"

"Ew, don't gross me out!"

"You know what I mean."

"So what do you know?"

"I know that. . . ."

"You know that what?"

"I know that he. . . ."

"You know that he what? Jesus."

"I know that he's got. . . ."

"Oh, my God. He tested positive. I don't believe it. Yes, I do. When was this?"

"Yesterday."

"Oh, my God. Jesus. How is he?"

"Pretty upset. I think he's going to go on the drugs."

"Oh, Jesus. I don't believe it. Yes, I do. I totally believe it."

"What are you saying?"

"I'm saying. . . . Oh, come on, as if you didn't know."

"Know what?"

"Know that he had his fucking legs in the air every night."

"Really?"

"Oh, yes, it's true."

"How do you know?"

"I have sources. I know somebody who goes to the baths regularly. He sees him there, like, practically *every* night. They've practically named a room after him."

"Ew. I could never go there."

"Neither could I. But some people, you know, they bring it on themselves."

"How can you say that? It's awful to say that."

"Nobody will say it publicly. It's too politically incorrect. But it's *true*."

"Well, you remember what Bette Davis said when they found Joan Crawford dead?"

"No, I don't, actually."

"This is her — Bette Davis. . . . How's this for a Bette Davis face?"

"*Very* good."

"Here goes. She said, 'I always try to say something good about the dead. So, Joan Crawford's dead. Good.'"

"Oh, you evil, evil man, that's awful."

"It's very funny, though."

"Yes, it is."

Fifth Prison Letter from Cindy Lou Williams

Dear Kasper,

I'm calling you that because I feel it's time. You feel these things. You feel them in your bones. Like rheumatism. Like my mother's arthritis, I guess.

I think that it's time for me to call you by your first name because I've learned something very important about you, something that makes you more human to me. And in the midst of all the incredible hustle and bustle of the last few days, it means even more.

First of all, let me say that I had no idea of the heinous nature of your crime or of the enormity of this case. For two weeks now, there have been small stories about the "AIDS KILLER." But as you well know (or do they let you have papers in there?), now that the testimony of the witnesses is about to begin, and the lawyers will be presenting their opening arguments, it has, well, suddenly blown open. They say that you may have killed *hundreds* of people!

They say that you may be the most dangerous serial killer in all history! They call you the "Human Epidemic" and the "Walking Plague"! And the descriptions of your physical person — well, I won't go into them here in case you haven't actually read them. Suffice it to say that the press is being very cruel.

After all, you are a human being. Somewhere you have a soul. As a matter of fact, I think I've found it. And I certainly know what it's like to be ridiculed for physical abnormalities. Let me tell you, my lifeless hair and my tendency to roundness in both face and figure have made me the butt of many cruel jokes by heartless boys in this particular town! It doesn't matter what you think of a person, it's not fair to criticize them for something that they cannot help. I cannot help my metabolism — or the inheritance of my mother's limp, straight hair — just as I'm sure that you are not to blame for your evil ways. Don't ask me how I know this, but I just do. One of the reasons that I have faith in your immortal soul (does not the Lord himself say that all will be forgiven?) is your recently revealed obsession with reading and knowledge. In this, you and I are quite alike. So alike that I can safely say I feel a bond with you. And I am hoping that this bond will lead to your salvation.

Your letter was short, but I could read between the lines. You have asked me to get you books. Again, I do not know the prison rules, but I will do my best. You say that in the prison library there are no copies of the Bible and no copies of *The Fountainhead*. I find this ironic in a kind of risible way. (As you can see, I've been using my dictionary. There's a great book for you!) Well, first of all, I can see nothing wrong at all with you reading both of those books, over and over. One could take worse books to a desert island! After all, in case you're not aware, both the Bible and *The Fountainhead* are best-sellers.

I will take both to you. And I will do my best to find the books that you have asked for. Oh, mother's calling, so I will end here. I know that you also mentioned The Phantom Anesthetist of Altoona or, as my grandmother used to call him, "The Gasser." My next letter will be about him.

Kasper, I may be the only one who cares about your immortal soul. I really do.

Keep smiling.

Yours,

Cindy Lou Williams

What Happened

Herein will be told what happened. How it happened. When it happened. And why I'm now in big trouble.

As you can probably see, there's a pattern. Yes, I've been killing a lot of people, just for fun. That's one pattern.

The other pattern is that I started off by killing people I hated and then gradually moved on to people I loved and cared about. Murder, like sex, is addictive. It's hard to do it "just a little bit." That's also why people get married and become monogamous, actually. They know that, if they try to have "just a little bit" of sex outside marriage, then it'll become too appealing. And they'll have to do it a lot. Sex is like heroin and murder. And just like Jeffrey Dahmer, who started out killing cats, I started out killing stupid drag queens. With Alphonse, I moved on to bigger game. The next logical step was to kill someone very special, someone with a lot of potential, someone I really, really loved.

To kill someone really beautiful.

Which brings me to Aaron Bucolic. His name has been changed, of course, to protect the innocent. And, yes, he was innocent. Very, very innocent. A beautiful little hero, actually.

In Aaron, I met my perfect match.

He was a perfect victim. Born to be a casualty, to die. Aren't we all? Yes, but some of us more than others. . . . He wore his death elegantly and with a kind of disdain. For Aaron, it wasn't important that death was his perfume, but it did make a difference to those around him.

The first thing you noticed about Aaron was his incredible fragility. The second thing was his eyes.

Of course, he was very thin. Except for the slightest swell of a belly. A belly that he was very ashamed of, actually. His arms were slender and hairless, the arms of a teenage girl. He had a long body, a long cock. Practically no ass.

He moved like a girl, but he wasn't effeminate in that nauseating way most of the fags in my building are effeminate. It almost seems as though they've read some book about what being a fag means. The first chapter is "How to Be Effeminate." And they know that means Bette Davis imitations (for the older ones) and Alanis Morissette imitations (for Aaron's friends). When these lousy fags are effeminate, it's a huge campy cry for attention. It's all about living out their gayness and showing it to the whole world, about being as gay as they can possibly be. It's annoying artifice with no centre — just mushy marshmallow cream that gives you indigestion.

Aaron was a woman. Except that he had a cock. He had all the grace and beauty, the kindness and weakness, the fragility and sweetness of a girl. He didn't play it up. He didn't *act* "campy." He just *was*. I remember, when I was dating him, stupid people would say to me, "Why are you dating him? You might as well date a girl." But, you see, I wasn't. I was dating Aaron.

The fragility was apparent not only in his body but also in the fact that he was sick all the time. With something. Oh, my God. He must have had thousands of AIDS tests. Doctors just loved him. He stepped into their offices, and they pounced. "A victim." Their little constipated doctor brains got all gummy with enthusiasm.

"Oh, my God, he looks so sick. So weak. And he's obviously homosexual. He must be dying. Oh, goody. Let's give him a test. He'll probably die. But I can do my best to save him. It'll be fun!" Aaron never had a family doctor — his parents were always moving around — so every time he had an ache or a pain — which was every other day — he made the trip to some little clinic. Doctors always gave him AIDS tests, and he always came back negative. They got all frantic. Their constipated little gummy brains thought, "He's so gay. So weak. So ill. And he doesn't have AIDS. Hmmm. How weird. Well, *something* is killing him!"

So then they'd give him a test for gonorrhea.

I remember that Aaron once went to the doctor for an ingrown toenail, and for some reason the doctor wanted to look in his throat. (Doctors can talk you into anything — after all, they went to medical school, you didn't!) He looked in and said, "Oh, my God." The doctor was horrified peering down this young homosexual's throat.

"What is it?" asked Aaron.

"Have you been engaging in oral sex?" asked the doctor, trying to be as polite as possible.

"Why, yes, I have," said Aaron in that calm, quiet, proud way he had. He wasn't ashamed of anything, and he couldn't help but be honest.

"Oh, my God."

"What is it?" asked Aaron, scared.

"I think you've got gonorrhea!" said the horrified doctor.

"No, it's probably strep throat," said Aaron cheerfully. He always had strep throat. He didn't really feel like Aaron when he *didn't* have it, actually. He was pleased to have strep throat. It meant he could take antibiotics. Aaron loved taking antibiotics, and doctors loved giving them to him. They took one look at Aaron and had an irresistible urge to prescribe antibiotics.

"Oh, my God!" said the doctor, still horrified at seeing such a young girly homosexual's obviously reddened and irritated throat. "Do you know who your sexual partners are, young man?"

"Not usually," said Aaron. He was a little slut and quite proud of it, but again in a quiet way.

"Oh, my God!" The doctor couldn't control himself. Although a deeply religious man, he was compelled by the sight to take the Lord's name in vain. "You've probably got that new strain of African gonorrhea! It's resistant to antibiotics! You'd better stop having sex altogether!"

"I probably won't stop having sex altogether," said Aaron.

"But you should!" said the doctor. "You should *for your health!*"

It was a dilemma that many doctors got into with Aaron. He walked into their offices looking like an AIDS victim, but he just *didn't* test positive. So they tested him for every other venereal disease they could think of. "This little girly thing just has to be infected!" their constipated gummy doctor brains reasoned.

Anyway, as usual, this doctor prescribed antibiotics. But after all the horror of looking at a young proud girly homosexual's throat up close, he forgot to look at Aaron's ingrown toenail.

His toenail got worse. But Aaron had lots of antibiotics to take, and he quite enjoyed taking them. He was always about to take, or had just taken, or had just forgotten to take a pill. "Did I take my pill just now?" he'd ask. Sometimes I'd lie and say no when he had. I figured he could always use two.

Aaron also had lots of sleeping pills and sedatives and Prozac. Although of calm demeanour, he was very tense and frightened and prone to anxiety and depression. A doctor's dream.

And then there were his eyes.

It's hard to describe them. I'd like to say he had the kindest eyes I've ever seen. They were the eyes of a pretty young girl who expected only the best from life. I remember introducing Aaron to somebody once who said, "That boy has the *kindest* face I have ever seen." He meant the kindest *eyes.*

I met Aaron on the steps of New York University. I used to hang around there sometimes looking for cute young guys to kill. And one day, sure enough, Aaron came bouncing down the steps with his little backpack. So adorable, he stopped, looked at me, and then sat opposite me to read a book. It was obvious he wanted me to talk to him.

You might wonder, if this boy was so young and light-haired and slender with light eyes, why he'd want to have anything to do with a Quasimodo look-alike.

Good question. Aaron, you see, like many pretty boys, had a kink. And it's those kinks that always get them involved with slightly older, less attractive men and often with deformed monsters like me. Aaron's kink was, quite simply, unattractive guys. Rubbies, actually. Now, I know that doesn't sound too likely, so let me be more explicit. (Kinks are always explicit.) Apparently, that first day, I was sporting two things that are particularly appealing to Aaron: bad teeth and a ripped hat. That's absolutely all it took to get his attention.

Part of my misshapenness is related to my old, decrepit, crooked teeth. I'm missing a tooth on each side — never bothered to have them filled in — and I've got one in the very front that desperately needs a cap. I'd never get it capped now, it brought me Aaron. I was also wearing an old, smelly, ripped hat that day. And Aaron, possibly because of the perfection of his fragile beauty, has always been perversely attracted to guys who look a little messed up. Guys who have tattoos, bad hats, and bad teeth. I looked a little rough to Aaron. But, of course, I am.

So he studied his book, and I studied him. Now and then he looked up and studied me back. Finally, I wandered over and started chatting him up.

He said he was studying creative writing and was impressed that I'm a painter. I told him that if he wanted to come over to my place I'd show him my book. We didn't have sex right away. I showed him my painting; he showed me his scribbled poetry. We circled each other, the way animals do. We knew that, if it happened, it would be a big thing.

It wasn't long before I figured out why Aaron fell so hard for me. He came from a "liberal" background. His parents were white and middle class and "nice." You know the type. The kind of people who think their shit doesn't stink. Actually, his father didn't shit. He'd had an operation and was left with a colostomy bag. He was some sort of diplomat who'd recently retired to the country because of asthma. Aaron's mother was a do-gooder, a philanthropist. Aaron was sent to school in Switzerland while they toured the world. Upon graduation, he got to tour the world by himself. He got into quite a bit of trouble, actually.

I should tell you about Aaron getting beaten up.

Which time? Which time should I tell you about? Aaron was always getting beaten up. Just like he was always getting prescribed antibiotics. He looked like a little lost boy/girl. And just as doctors saw him as AIDS waiting to happen, thugs saw him as an invitation to gay-bashing. His attraction to scuzzy-looking types didn't help.

In Italy after graduation, Aaron couldn't help hanging around the Coliseum at night, trying to suck off some low-life Italian dick. Well, some of those Italian types are very uptight about their masculinity, and one of the boys he approached was such a closet case that he beat up Aaron after the fabulous blowjob he received. I know that Aaron gave him a fabulous blowjob because he always gave fabulous blowjobs. But the amazing thing was that after that incident Aaron went out the next week, to the *same place,* and gave *somebody else* a blowjob. He would have gone sooner, but he was too weak to walk. As soon as he could walk, he was back there on his knees behind some Roman ruin, getting ruined by some Roman. This was typical. Just as he sort of threw himself into his sicknesses, he threw himself into dangerous situations on purpose.

But, you know, I didn't see it as stupid. Even if his parents did.

Aaron told me that the way his mother used to put her hand on his shoulder and say "Be smart. Be safe" drove him crazy. The words actually made him want to risk getting really sick or badly beaten up.

I saw Aaron as a hero.

Yeah, the world is filled with goofs who want to kill you just because you're gay. And it's filled with doctors who treat you like a lab experiment: "Why don't you try AZT? If it doesn't kill you, then it will save you!"

Aaron knew this.

He knew how horrible and scary the world is, how sadistic people just wanted to get their claws into a little victim like him. Instead of being afraid, though, he walked right into it, over and over again. He walked right into every doctor's office and alley. And he walked right into me. I guess it was partially to overcome his fear. He knew that, if he ever became too afraid of doctors or thugs, he might never leave the house. But there was also a thrill in being afraid and in conquering that fear. That's why he'd walk right into the headlights, his fragile head held high.

This complicated our life together. Aaron's youthful, gay-lib enthusiasm, and his zest for confronting fear, manifested itself in his need to be affectionate with me in public. Affectionate with the Hunchback of Notre Dame.

I remember the Christmas after we first met. It was when we decided we *loved* each other. We were both pretty scared of saying that word. Aaron didn't know why I was scared. That if I said I loved him I might also want to kill him. So he'd kid me about it.

"Kasper, why can't you say it? Why can't you say the word?"

I'd say, "I like you very, very much Aaron."

And then he'd say, "Very, very, very much?"

"Very, very, very, very much."

And then he'd ask, "How many 'veries' does it take to make love?"

And I'd tell him that I wasn't sure. Because I wasn't.

But then one night — during the first snowfall of the year, in front of Macy's Christmas windows — it was just too touching. I thought, "I can't censure myself. I mean, how can I be sure that saying I love him *out loud* is going to make me want to kill him? Besides, killers need love to." So I held him in my arms and kissed him and said, "Okay, we can say it now. We can say 'I love you.'"

And some stupid family was standing there by the windows. They looked pitiful. Very poor — recent immigrants from somewhere. And when I kissed Aaron, I swept him off the ground (I was a lot bigger than he was; it was quite awful looking, I'm sure). The father and mother suddenly huddled their kids close and shielded their eyes from the horror of our very public love. Then they quickly hurried their kids away, the baby in the stroller too. I remember thinking that maybe the baby in the stroller was gay. That little baby (I don't know if it was a boy or a girl) sure stared at us. But it was probably just because he — let's call it a boy — knew his mother didn't want him to stare. Right?

That night Aaron's bravery tested my limits. The kiss was just an impulsive thing. But when the immigrant family scurried away in fear, *I* was scared. Big ugly killer Kasper was scared. Okay, I wasn't really scared. I just realized, even though I'm a killer, that I don't delight in scaring children. I draw the line there.

"Maybe we should have gone somewhere else to kiss."

"No," said Aaron. "Kiss me again. Here."

So we kissed in front of the Christmas windows again, the first light snow falling gently around us. I'm sure we scared other wholesome families. I'm sure a husband turned to his wife and said, "Gaylib is one thing, but why do they have to ruin Christmas?"

And the wife probably said, "And that larger man was so ugly!"

"Well, they're not all Calvin Klein models, you know. Contrary to popular misconception."

And then they probably wheeled their kiddies away, shielding more young eyes.

So we made a spectacle of ourselves that night because Aaron just had to walk right into homo-haters, right into the middle of all the shit.

And that's what made him a hero to me.

He was a little fragile guy, but he wasn't afraid to take all the shit that got thrown on his thin little shoulders.

Deciding to kill him makes me feel bad now.

But he wanted it, expected it, and, like all the others, deserved it.

Sixth Prison Letter from Cindy Lou Williams

Dear Kasper,

So, tomorrow's the big day! I'm so excited. I know that I won't sleep tonight.

I wonder what it's like for you, all alone in your cell. Tomorrow I'm going to bring some books. I'm also going to ask if it's all right for me to meet with you.

You must be relieved, at least, that things are finally going to start.

For what it's worth, I don't believe that you attempted to murder all those boys. And how are they going to prove their case? It seems to me that, if you attempted murder, then you must have wanted to kill *all* of them. That I can't imagine. In your letters (which I will always treasure), you have proved yourself to be an intelligent man. No one could be as sensitive as you and purposely kill people. You must have just forgotten the "important safety measures for those intimate moments." It's very difficult for me to talk about these things — I'm sure that you know what I mean! In fact, I know that I'm going to be covering my ears often in the courtroom.

Now, I promised you a story, and that's what you're going to get. So curl up nice and comfy, because this is good.

I mentioned that I did a lot of research when I tried to write a report on the June Bug Epidemic. In the end, I wrote about the "Psychohistory of Mass Hysteria" with the help of that nice Miss Kramm. Well, during my reading, I came across the tale of The Phantom Anesthetist of Altoona. As soon as I saw this, I ran home to talk to my grandmother. My paternal grandmother was the real head of our family. She lived upstairs, and even though she hardly ever came downstairs — she had very bad arthritis — she pretty well ruled with an iron hand. Anyway, Altoona is a little town in Pennsylvania. I knew that because it's the town from which my grandmother hails. Of course, I just had to ask her about The Phantom Anesthetist.

It turned out that she knew all about it from personal experience!

You see, my own great-grandmother had come under the hand of the anesthetist. (Granny preferred to call him The Gasser.)

Altoona was a small town at the turn of the century. It was mainly famous for growing tomatoes, sleepy summer afternoons, and the big houses in town that were built by the Tomato King — John Jacob Rutledge.

Well, Great-Granny Mitlinger, that's what we called her, was fast asleep one July night in one of those big Altoona tomato mansions, having herself a wonderful sleep. Great-Grandpa Mitlinger was beside her, of course, in their big oak bed. He was a sound sleeper, and he had no trouble at all sleeping through Great-Granny's snoring. He was so used to it that it actually put him to sleep. Well, this particular hot summer night (it was actually more like early morning), to his surprise, Great-Granny Mitlinger suddenly stopped snoring. Soon after, Great-Grandpa awoke (from the lack of regular noise) and looked beside him. Where Great-Granny usually slept, there was nothing but a very deep indentation. (She had a tendency to plumpness; I have unfortunately inherited that particular affliction from her side of the family!). Great-Grandpa Mitlinger was very upset. Great-Granny was his one true love — they were married when she was only 17 — and he was very protective of her. So he wrapped himself in his great purple robe and rushed downstairs. And what do you think he found there?

I'll bet you could never guess!

He found Great-Granny Mitlinger standing in front of the window — of *the parlour* — which was, of course, the best, most special room in the house, the room used only for guests. You see, the window faced Wittlemeyer Street, which was the main street of the town. And there was Great-Granny standing on the back of the massive couch doing some sort of dance! Great-Grandpa later described it as the hootchie kootchie. Great-Granny was swishing and waving as if she were an Arabian chorus girl! There was no music, she was dancing to a tune that only she could hear. And then she did an even more bizarre thing. She turned her back to the window and lifted up her nightdress and exposed her ample fanny to the whole town. Unfortunately, at that moment, Gus the milkman was making his morning rounds. He caught sight of Great-Granny Mitlinger's gigantic bum, which nearly filled the plate-glass picture window. Great-Grandpa saw Gus stop his horse and just gaze at her, his mouth agape with surprise. Well, as you might imagine, Great-Grandpa ran over to the window and pulled the curtains and tried to pull Great-Granny Mitlinger down. She wouldn't budge, and she just kept dancing. Finally, the only thing that he could do was slap her. She let out a blood-curdling scream. It woke up the whole house, including my grandmother, who ran downstairs. Unfortunately, my grandmother appeared just in time to witness Great-Granny Mitlinger rolling around on top of Great-Grandpa and trying desperately to strangle him. Grandma ran over and separated them, which was no easy feat. She had to keep repeating Great-Granny's name over and over. That's what finally stopped her. "Minnie Saloops!" she said. "Minnie Saloops! Stop! Stop!" "Saloops" was Great-Granny Mitlinger's maiden name. Finally, Great-Granny stopped strangling her husband.

When everyone had calmed down, Great-Granny Mitlinger was questioned. She claimed to have been in a trance. She didn't remember dancing in the window. She didn't remember being slapped by Great-Grandpa. And she didn't remember strangling him either. The only thing that she remembered was her daughter's voice yelling "Minnie Saloops!" Great-Grandpa and his daughter were confused. What could possibly have caused Great-Granny to go into a trance? That's when my grandmother thought she smelled something. She followed the smell (she always had a good sense of smell, and it made her a maniac about cleanliness) up to her parents' bedroom. Upstairs, it was much more intense. The odour was unfamiliar — strange — perhaps a poisonous gas. It made them all very nervous, and no one could get back to sleep.

The next day, Great-Grandpa went to the Altoona police and informed them of the incident. Gus had already mentioned the window display! The next night, the whole family went to bed with fans in their windows to blow away any noxious fumes that might catch them unawares.

Well, Great-Granny slept well that second night, and there was no more dancing in the window. But the next day, when she had her regular Tuesday tea with Mrs. Bloomfield, she discovered that she wasn't the only one to have experienced a weird and almost tragic twist of fate. It turned out that Mrs. Bloomfield's sister, Nellie, had also been dancing late at night, and again there had been a smell — the Bloomfields thought that it was sulfur!

Sulfur!

At first, people suspected that it was some sort of witchcraft. But Nellie's husband found flowers crushed in the garden outside their bedroom window.

And thus was born the legend of The Phantom Anesthetist of Altoona.

After that, it became a real epidemic. No fewer than *twenty* women in Altoona fell prey to The Gasser. The town became frantic. No one knew when or where The Gasser would strike next. The effects of his gas were basically the same. Only the dances that the women performed were different. They all, however, ended up trying to strangle their husbands until they were forcibly woken up — always by someone shouting their maiden names! But before they awoke, some of them really hurt their husbands. One of the husbands almost died of asphyxiation and had trouble speaking for the rest of his life.

As you might have suspected, Kasper, since this story was in my book about mass hysteria, they never found The Phantom Gasser. Some thought that it was Ernie, the semiretarded gas pump attendant who certainly had access to lots of noxious spirits. Others suspected Mr. Kriks, the academy chemistry teacher. Still others, for spurious reasons, I think, accused the only Jewish person in town, Simon Glassman. Glassman had no access to any noxious spirits or chemicals whatsoever, but he'd made what many thought was an obnoxious amount of money from boxing and shipping tomatoes north.

Was there ever a gasser? Or was it, as my schoolbook says, a case of mass hysteria? I guess we'll never know for sure. But for almost a month, it held the inhabitants of a small Pennsylvania town in thrall.

Good story, isn't it? Well, if this hasn't put you to sleep already, then I wish you a good night!

I'll see you in court tomorrow. I'll wear my special kitten pin, so you'll be sure to see me.

Your friend and inveterate letter writer,
Cindy Lou Williams

What Happened

You probably don't want to hear about how and why I tried to kill the one boy I loved, but you're going to hear it anyway. It'll be good for you.

Eat your broccoli.

You might find it strange that I loved Aaron at all, that I loved him for being so brave in the face of all the homophobes. I mean, I'm sort of a homophobe myself.

Okay, let me clear that up. I don't hate all homosexuals. I hate just the stupid ones. I don't kill all homosexuals. Just the stupid, worthless ones who deserve to die. Which, I admit, is quite a few of them.

I am so ruthless that I sometimes kill homosexuals who are stupid for *just one moment.*

You can never let down your guard, you know.

And, for all his courage, Aaron could be really stupid too. After all, nobody's perfect.

When was Aaron stupid? Well, he was stupid when he talked about his stomach. Now, look at me — literally the Hunchback — and imagine what it might be like to listen to skinny little Esmeralda whining on about her tummy. Her bulging tummy! Okay, Aaron's tummy bulged a *teensy* bit. But it was a sweet, gentle boy bulge. It wasn't a huge sack of potatoes like my gargantuan hairy bag of guts. Maybe he shaved it, I don't know, but when I kissed his tummy it was as sweet as an apple and just as smooth.

No, stupid, I didn't kill him for whining about his tummy. The tummy thing was only the beginning. When it started, it was the first sign that he was embarking on a binge of wallowing — self-pity in spades.

There was a lot of shit for Aaron to wallow in. His physical and mental health was always precarious. And then there were the trances. Now and then, he'd go into trances when he was asleep.

He called it a nervous disorder. Sleepwalking. I noticed that episodes occurred when he was going through a period of low self-esteem. Now, Aaron *always* talked in his sleep. Mostly, it was about being attacked.

"No . . . no . . . get away from me!" he'd shout, tossing his little blond head on the pillow. "No . . . no, please don't!"

When I first heard him do that, I was freaked out. I asked him about it, and he told me that the important thing was not to touch him when he was in that state.

"So you are dreaming about being attacked?"

"Usually — I think so," said Aaron.

But sometimes it was worse. Sometimes he didn't stay in bed, he'd get up and walk around saying, "No . . . no . . . get away." Sometimes, like this, he'd wreck his apartment. I think he was trying to defend himself. When I first saw his place, I wondered why it was so messy. Later I figured it was because he regularly trashed it in his sleep and didn't always have the time to clean it up.

Anyway, never mind, why bother?

So, when he was in one of these sleepwalking, bad-body-image periods, he was also very promiscuous.

Aaron and I didn't have one of those monogamous relationships. We weren't as stupid as that. I mean, I've always enjoyed having different guys chew on my cock. And Aaron always liked to suck on lots of different cocks. No problem. I was never the kind of guy who wanted to keep his lover from going out and having fun. At least not until I met Aaron.

The thing was, I was so serious about Aaron that I began to get jealous. Let me tell you something about jealousy: it can turn you into a maniac.

Aaron and I didn't see each other every night or anything. Just a few times a week. On other nights, the deal was, well, *never ask*. He knew I went out and got a little dirty sex, and I knew he did the same thing. Fine. We didn't want to know any more than that.

One night I phoned him, and he sounded really weird. Like he wanted me to get off the phone, which wasn't usual. I don't know why I wouldn't hang up. I swear, with any other asswipe whom I just *happened* to be fucking, I probably would have taken the hint. But I was so crazy for little Aaron — so crazy in love with him — that I just couldn't leave it alone.

"So what's going on?"

"Oh, I'm going out."

"Out where?"

"Nowhere special."

This is the time when, if you're a sensible, mature homosexual, you stop asking. "Nowhere special" is code for "Don't ask." But Aaron was making me crazy. His little victim arms, his beautiful victim eyes. . . . But he was my victim. I didn't want anyone else to have him.

"Where 'nowhere'?"

"Nowhere."

"Who you going with?"

"A friend."

"What friend?"

"Oh, no one. You don't know him."

"I know everybody."

"Umm . . . I don't think you know this guy."

"Try me. What's his name?"

"His name?" (He paused.) "His name is Jeff."

"Oh yeah? Jeff who?" Now I was really acting like an asshole. A typical jealous homosexual. But I just couldn't stop. "So who is this Jeff?" I pressed.

"Oh, a friend."

"You've never mentioned him to me."

"No, I never have."

"Why?"

"Hey, I don't mention *everybody* to you."

"So who is this guy?"

"Just a guy."

"This isn't a date, is it?"

"*Kasper.*"

"What?"

"Why are you asking me all this?"

"I just want to know."

"Listen. I've got to go. Can we talk about it tomorrow?"

"No, I want to talk about it now."

"Kasper."

"What does he look like?"

"I'm not going to tell you what he — "

"Is he a little guy like you?"

"No, he's not little."

"Is he a big ugly guy like me?"

"No, he's not like you. And you're not ugly."

"What does he look like?"

"Well, he's sort of . . . muscular."

"Muscular? This guy is muscular? Is he a muscle guy? Hey, is this a date?"

"Look. I've got to go. I'll talk to you tomorrow. I love you, Kasper."

And then he hung up. My little victim boy hung up on me. Jesus, I was so fucking mad. The last thing he managed to tell me is that Jeff — oh, God, I hate that name, that perfect name, *Jeff* — is a fucking "muscular" guy? I hate that. I hate that word. *Muscular.* Something I'll never be. I'll never be muscular. I'll always be a big guy. But no one will ever see my muscles. Of course, I've *got* them — but they're hiding under layers of fat and ugly hairy flesh. All I could think about that night was little Aaron getting pressed into the bed by this horrible muscular Jeff character. I mean, they probably did things that he and I *never* did. Aaron was probably licking the guy's ass. He never licked my huge dirty smelly ass. But he was probably licking this guy's perfect muscular butt. My God, I was going crazy. If I were a sleepwalker like Aaron, I'd have wrecked my whole apartment.

The next day Aaron was so mature about it that I wanted to kill him.

"So let's talk about last night," he said.

"Yeah," I said, "I guess we should." Couldn't he see that it was the only damn thing I wanted to talk about? But it was the very last thing I wanted to talk about too.

"You seemed to be fishing for information."

"Oh, did I?"

"Yes, Kasper. I thought we had an agreement."

"We do."

"I thought we agreed that we had an open relationship and that we weren't going to talk about who we are fucking on the side."

"So you're fucking him?"

"Who?"

"Don't act stupid. This Jeff guy."

"Kasper, I don't understand why you're so upset. We agreed."

We were sitting in Aaron's kitchen. Right then I turned around, and there, on his fridge, was Jeff's phone number. I swear, Jeff's *card*. I couldn't believe it. Whoever this guy was, he had the audacity to have *a card*. And there it was, stuck right up there with a little gay flag fridge magnet — oh, how I hate those stupid gay flags, but I hate fridge magnets even more — along with the telephone numbers of Aaron's school and the pharmacy where he got all his antibiotics. There was no profession written on the card, of course. Nothing like "Jeff Marshall, Plumber." That would have been funny. Or "Jeff Marshall, Right Good Fuck." No, it didn't say anything like that. It just said "Jeff Marshall." Hey, nobody has a business card with *no profession* on it. Except hookers. He was probably a hooker. That was it. Aaron was seeing a hooker and *not paying*. Oh, shit, I hate it when beautiful boys —

who usually make older, uglier guys like me pay — get together and have fun. It makes me really fucking mad. At that moment, I hated Aaron. I hated him for snaring me with his fragile beauty.

Well, we'd see how fragile that beauty could really be.

I hated his perfect, white-boy sensibleness. I hated it that he was so adjusted and that he'd been to so many gay-lib group therapy meetings that he could calmly sit in front of his ugly old boyfriend and say, "Didn't we have an arrangement? Don't you understand?" I hated reasonableness. I hated his pale skin. But most of all, I hated his understanding, intelligent, mature family. His perfect father, the diplomat with the colostomy bag, and his mother, the ever-so-open-minded liberal who drove him nutty with her well-meaning cautions.

It was then that I decided to kill him.

"Oh, never mind," I said.

"Really?" said Aaron, his pretty blue eyes alight with surprise.

"Hey, I'm being unreasonable."

"It's just . . . we had an agreement. And we said we wouldn't pry. You know you're my special one. My big bear guy."

That's what he always called me. His big bear guy.

Yeah, that was okay. Things were fine. No problem.

"Forget I ever asked."

There was no more talk about Jeff.

But I nurtured it. My hurt. It was very important to me, very dear. I mean, I'd have liked to get rid of it, but there was no way I could. Jeff had become an insurmountable rift. And, as much as I loved Aaron, it seemed to me that I'd always hate him too.

Killing Aaron wasn't difficult. For all his maturity, and gay-lib meetings, and brave confrontations of homophobia, and gay-lib pins, he was still self-hating. He'd get drunk on the nights when he was overcome with revulsion over his cute little "belly." So, one night when he was really, really drunk, I fucked him without a condom. It was easy. Just injected the ol' infected love juice. He didn't even know I did it. And I didn't feel bad afterward. Sure, at first I really fell for that slender little victim of homophobia and injustice. But gazing at Aaron through the prism of jealousy, his heroism suddenly resembled a sanctimonious pose.

I know you don't believe me. I know you believe I still love Aaron, despite what I did to him. And maybe I do. But I'm no suicide, okay? I had to kill somebody. And I didn't want to kill myself. I just couldn't look at Aaron anymore. And I couldn't bear him being happy without me, with some "Jeff" somewhere.

Soon after I did him in, his school term ended, and he went back to his home in Wyoming for the holidays. His parents had a ranch out there. It wasn't long before he had another AIDS test. Most little gayboys have one every other month, hoping to be part of the club. Hoping to become heroic, suffering victims like their older, gayer brothers.

Well, of course, Aaron tested positive, and of course he told his parents. Why not? I'm sure he thought that they'd say the right things. After all, they were a couple of diplomats. Still, they grilled him. And Aaron confessed.

Suddenly, the nice upper-middle-class couple lost all their niceness. All their "tolerance." Have you ever seen *Guess Who's Coming to Dinner?* It was that kind of thing. Oh yeah, they used to be happy that their son was gay. They used to handle it ever so well. Until Aaron got AIDS. Then they decided to charge the "perpetrator" with "attempted murder."

That's how I ended up in jail in Aaron's hometown. Kasper, Wyoming. A place with the same name as me. And why I started getting letters from this crazy broad named Cindy Lou Williams. She is so in love with me that it makes me sick.

Now I guess you're going to want to hear about the trial.

My Trial

It was a farce. A *complete* farce. I expected it to be bad but not *that* bad.

I mean, first of all, I was tried in Wyoming for something that had occurred in New York. This didn't make any sense to me, but apparently it's legal — I was charged in Wyoming.

Since I'm an evil killer, trying me in Wyoming made a lot of sense. It's the Wild West. And I have to admit that I was thrilled about being tried in Wyoming for two reasons.

First, I'd always wanted to visit the west, and I figured I'd get what was coming to me: hanging, dismemberment by horses, that sort of thing.

Second, I'd get to see Aaron on his home turf.

It was a real kick seeing him again there. Did I tell you how white his skin is? It's absolutely the palest skin I've ever seen. Aaron *cannot* go out in the sun. When he went to Italy, he wore a big straw hat. I remember, especially, the skin of his armpits, soft and a bit fuzzy, warm and a bit sour. I'd spent many a night with my head buried in there. I watched him sitting behind the prosecuting attorney with his parents, and my love for him seemed to erase the hate. I missed him, and I was sorry that I had to kill him. I thought that, maybe if I got on the stand and talked about his armpits, they'd have to let me off. I mean, what could be crazier? Because that was the issue here: whether I was a crazy killer (who belonged in a hospital) or a sane one (who deserved to be skinned alive and then barbecued).

Besides, in Wyoming there was no sign of Jeff, who was sort of a New York thing, so in a weird way I had Aaron all to myself. That's the thing about loving someone — you'll do anything to keep him for yourself.

I'm going to tell you about all the jurors. Each and every one. I'm going to tell you what they do in bed and what fucks them up

— what makes them scared at night. Because it was those two things that had the most influence on their decision.

If you're wondering how I found out about their personal lives, well, it all has to do with somebody who's had a pretty big effect on me: Miss Cynthia Louise Williams.

Anyway, my jury was a real societal cross section. People from every walk of life, a fair representation of Wyoming's citizenry.

I really mean it. I got exactly what I deserved. I won't put myself above Kasper, Wyoming. I am Kasper, and Kasper is me. We're one and the same thing.

I need you to get into each twisted brain involved in my case. The brains of the judge and the prosecuting attorney — two really fucked-up brains. And the brains of all twelve jurors. There's not much to say about my defence attorney except that he was a nice liberal guy whose big mistake was to believe I was innocent.

I'd tell him, "Hey, I'm guilty. I'm ugly and evil, and I did it."

And he'd say, "You don't mean that. You're just a little mentally unbalanced."

But I'll give him one thing: he did let me get on the stand and tell my story.

About the jurors, let me just say that they fell into two categories. There were the ones who decided from the start that I was guilty, victims of their own little Kasperian prejudices. The others? They went through a certain amount of agonized soul searching before they came up with a verdict.

The Private Life of Juror 1

Lorena Mady Kelly sat in the front corner of the jury box. She wore a perfect white bow in her hair and dresses with lovely white collars and white *gloves*. I bet you'd find her in church wearing a hat. She wore a lot of makeup, especially foundation. Lorena was very pretty except for the crow's-feet. She always sat up straight, and her cute little knees pressed together like a vise. I tried to catch her eye all the time. It was very difficult. She drove me absolutely crazy. Lorena Mady Kelly was a work of art.

Her father's family, the Madys, were considered the "Kennedys" of Kasper. In a town like Kasper, having a long lineage means, basically, one thing: your ancestors were killers. But I don't think Lorena looked at it in that way. As far as she was concerned, her family was "old blood." She always pointed to the fact that one of her ancestors ("Mad Mady") defended Platte Bridge with Kaspar Collins [sic], the town's heroic namesake. Lorena wasn't going to let anyone in town forget her family's accomplishments, however spurious they were.

Nabbing Jack Kelly for a husband added another feather in her ancestral cap. The Kellys were old Kasperians too, proudly descended from liars and killers. Jack's great-grandfather, Tom Horn, murdered ten ranchers. When the Madys and the Kellys got together, it was a union of two royal houses, two classic killer family lines.

Now, there wasn't much love between Lorena and Jack. At first, they were passionate because, well, everybody believed they *should* be. But Jack was a dedicated alcoholic, a man who didn't need to work because his father had made a fortune in Mace. Lorena was singularly interested in parties. God, Lorena could throw a party — for anything.

She'd had two children: the first had died of spinal meningitis. She was left with Albert Kelly, her second born. The family hope. Except. . . .

Albert was one of the few openly gay sons of Kasper.

Basically, Lorena hated fags. My God, she hated them. Luckily, her son wasn't at all like Aaron Bucolic. He wasn't a little, beautiful, sickly, political fag. He was a big, perfect, muscled, white boy. And unlike Aaron, he hadn't ended up in New York cruising Hunchback of Notre Dame look-alikes. No, Albert had gone to Harvard and met another perfect boy.

Albert Kelly and Ronald Metzger were the model gay couple of Boston. Both law students, both polite, handsome, cultured, and not at all "flamboyant." Everyone loved them. I'm sure that even straight boys wanted to hang out with them, you know, they were that masculine. Girls probably wanted to marry them both. And I'm sure everybody fantasized, secretly, about what they did in bed. When Cindy Lou told me about them, I was nauseated. Actually, she didn't say that Albert was a homosexual, but when she told me the details of his life it was pretty obvious.

I thought I'd have killed them both if I'd ever had the chance. But, then, neither of the perfect behemoths would have even looked at me sideways.

The plot thickened when Lorena Mady Kelly later organized a huge wedding for her niece, Brandy.

Brandy was a pretty, dumb girl whom I'm not going to talk about at all. I refuse to say anything about somebody named Brandy. You've got her name, isn't that enough? Anyway, the whole town was coming out to the wedding, and Lorena had gone nuts with pink. Everything was going to be pink — the cake, the gowns — they even found a Baptist church in town with a pink interior. The walls were stuccoed asbestos, but that didn't stop Lorena. They were the right colour! The wedding was going to be the biggest event in her party-holding career. Jack was just back from drying out in a Denver detox centre, so he was looking fabulous.

Yes, Lorena invited Albert to come, she even asked him to bring a "date."

Albert promised to attend the wedding.

How could he have thought he could go back home with his lover and not get killed? Well, when you've been living in a perfect postmodern world of Boston gay support and success, it's hard to remember that your family of inbred Midwestern killers are still consumed with hate.

Of course, Lorena expected Albert to bring a woman. She'd

sort of wiped her son's gayness from her mind. Mothers have a way of doing that. And, being a nice middle-class fag, Albert didn't really want to remind her of the bad news over and over again. Maybe he should have.

The only issue that plagued Albert and Ron was what to wear. Matching pink tuxedos would have been over the top. I'll bet Albert thought that they should both dress correctly and formally. And I'll bet Ron, in a crazy moment he'd later regret, suggested that they wear wild ties.

"Wild, what do you mean, wild, lover?" Albert would have asked suspiciously.

"Well, what about our Pooh and Piglet ties?" Ron might have coyly replied.

For their fifth anniversary, Ron had bought matching Disney Pooh Bear and Piglet ties. They were quite ugly. The Disney figures were, however, pink — which, fatally, would match Lorena's wedding colour.

"Do your mother a favour, dear," she probably said. "Wear something small and pink, will you?"

So Ron's suggestion, though outlandish (and, I'm sure, atypical of his usual good judgement), wasn't entirely inappropriate. Albert was probably hesitant because of the secret meaning of the Pooh and Piglet ties. A meaning that was, frankly, obscene. You see, in their sexual world, Ron and Albert had nicknamed each other Piglet and Pooh. Albert, who was slightly larger and had a very large, uncircumcised penis, was Pooh. Ron, who was slightly smaller and had a slightly smaller circumcised penis, was Piglet. Piglet often found himself sucking off Pooh and later being fucked by Pooh's thick dick. Sometimes Piglet was so overcome by emotion during coitus that he yelled, "Oh, Pooh. Fuck me, Pooh, please fuck me."

Okay, I made this part up about Albert and Ron. But it just seems so fucking *likely*.

So you can understand Albert's hesitation about the ties.

"But," I'm sure Ron argued in his best, persuasive lawyer style, "no one will know the *secret* meaning. Least of all Lorena, she will see them as cute and cuddly cartoon characters that fit in with her pink theme."

The day of the wedding, the two handsome young men looked gorgeous in their black tuxedoes. And all of Brandy's friends and relatives were charmed by them and, of course, by their cute, matching Disney-character ties.

Except for Lorena. She was murderous. Having conveniently forgotten that Albert was gay, the shock of his obvious gay coupledom, accentuated by the Piglet and Pooh ties, deeply humiliated her. She was so humiliated that all the warlike energies of the lawless cowboys in her Wild West background conspired to bring her emotions to the boiling point.

After the wedding, there was a grand, very pink reception at the Ramada. Lorena had rented a hospitality suite for herself and her family to use as a home base. When the reception ended, Lorena asked Albert to come upstairs to the hospitality suite for a talk.

After that discussion, no one saw Albert alive again.

He was strangled by Lorena in a hospitality suite. Strangled by his own mother, with his own Pooh tie. Some thought it odd that five-foot-four Lorena could have subdued her six-foot son. Odd to everyone, in fact, but Jack, who knew her ways.

Lorena was later sentenced to twelve years in prison. Her Kasperian jurors understood that there were extenuating circumstances.

Anyhow, all this happened a couple of years after my trial. Some *Enquirer* articles gave me all the juicy details. The pictures of Albert, dead, sporting a pink Pooh tie said it all. But it gives you an idea of what kind of woman Lorena was.

When she stared at me from the jury box and pressed her pink little knees together, I knew that she wanted me dead. I was like the monster version of her son, the nightmare she most feared, the

Hunchback who wilfully infected people with AIDS.

Anyway, Lorena Mady Kelly didn't prove to be a very sympathetic juror.

My Trial

As I mentioned, the trial was a farce. It was the job of the defence to prove that I was insane, so the big plan was to put me on the stand. It was the job of the prosecution to prove that I was an evil, malignant killer. They had it easy.

Consider my general appearance. As I've probably mentioned nine hundred times, I'm about as ugly as anyone you'll ever see. If you asked ten little kids to draw the most evil monster in the world, they'd all probably draw me. Sure, there are people in the world who think I'm attractive. Aaron, for instance, loved my greasy hair; rotting teeth; round, swollen-eyed, misshapen face; bad skin; mottled beard; baggy, semen-stained army pants; old T-shirt so transparent that you can see my hairy gut through it. Another thing: I don't smile. I never smile. Because when I do it's scarier than when I frown, you know?

I could see the jurors looking at me with, well, horror. I was exactly what they expected an AIDS killer to look like. Hey, I'll probably be the only person to play me in a movie — they'll never find anyone as ugly as me to do it!

One game I played to pass the time during the trial was to sit there staring at my dirty old pants and then quickly look up and catch one of the jurors — it could have been Lorena Mady Kelly or Ronald Heavyfeather, for instance — staring at me. It always freaked them out. And it made me seem a bit more crazy.

The prosecution's first tactic was to question every person who hated me. It wasn't hard to find volunteers.

Basically, I'm a hated person. Everyone hates me except for the couple of nutbars who actually *love* me. I mean, for one thing, I'm very cranky, and I don't wear a perpetual smile like most of the idiots in this universe. Why should I waste my time being friendly to stupid people? Most of the world is made up of stupid people, after all.

I hate nice, cheery, friendly people. When they say hi, usually out of pity because I'm so smelly and ugly, I usually just ignore them.

So they hauled out everybody. I mean everybody. The prosecution paid for them to come all the way from New York. Now, it was one thing when they hauled out The Vicious Teller and Robbie the Leather Guy; after all, I'd had physical altercations with them. It was really something else, though, when they dragged in The Street Girl, The Guy at the Store, and The Ugliest Guy Who Ever Set Foot in a Bathhouse.

The Vicious Teller was a great witness. I mean, the point was for the prosecution to show that I was calculating and evil, that I had a pattern of cruelty and violence in my life.

I know you're not supposed to call them tellers anymore. They all wear little badges these days that say "Customer Service Representative." Right. Fuck that. A teller is a teller. And those tellers never give me any service — at least not the kind I *need*. So, as far as I'm concerned, they're all fucking *tellers*.

The thing that was so great about this teller was that she looked so fucking beautiful and efficient. I don't know if you've ever noticed this about tellers, but they've got to be just the most beautiful people in the world. I'm sure they're chosen for their looks. Not so much the men (although a lot of fags end up being bank tellers — it's the most common job for Queens from Hell, next to florist, decorator, and window display designer). But the *women*! This one, she was Asian (I mention that only because it made her even more beautiful), with jet-black hair pulled straight back and black eyes and an incredible figure. Nice, juicy, little tits. And she always wore black satiny dresses with little lacy tops and a perfect red lipstick.

She was a knockout.

One day I went to her to cash a cheque. Maybe I should describe the bank.

Yeah, I should.

It was the ugliest little bank I've ever seen. Don't let anyone ever tell you that they don't put the ugliest banks in the worst neighbourhoods. So right next to my crummy, sad little drag queen building was this ugly bank. They hadn't painted the inside or hung a picture since 1955, which meant that everything was peeling and grey and institutional. Pitiful old landscapes hung on the walls. They'd spent money on only one thing: the tellers' windows were heavily barred and covered with bullet-proof glass. Hell, they didn't have anything to make the place pretty, but they sure had enough money for *that*. Not because they were afraid of *normal* crime, no sir. They were scared to death that one of the raging, AIDS-infected homosexuals from the building next door would spit on them. I swear, the tellers stood farther back from the counter — *and they were behind plate glass.* I mean, besides *Dog Day Afternoon*, when was the last time you saw a fag hold up a bank? I'm convinced they were just scared of getting physically close to us. I know you think I'm paranoid, but it was the only bank in the neighbourhood to have both bars *and* glass.

Well, I went to cash a cheque with this beautiful teller, and from the start she didn't pay any attention to me. Her window was empty, and I walked up, and it was a little game at the beginning — who was going to say hello first? And I thought, "*She* should say hello; after all, *I'm* the *fucking customer*." But not ultraslick Miss Suzy Wong, nosirree! So I stood there for what seemed like ten minutes and finally said, "Excuse me, I hope I'm not interrupting you?" I admit that it was a very obnoxious thing to say, but what killed me is that she didn't even react. Not even my incredible rudeness could faze her.

"I'll be with you in a minute," she said, not even looking up from whatever crap she was doing. Yeah, counting money. What could be more important than counting fucking money?

When she finally finished, she looked irritated that I'd interrupted her, and then she sighed as though the weight of the world was on her pretty little shoulders. She didn't even bother to smile.

"Can I help you?" she said. She really meant "Can I screw you?"

Which is exactly what she did.

So there I was, facing her behind bars *already*, behind a quarter-inch of bulletproof glass, in my stained T-shirt and jeans, looking very, well, fuckable, I guess, from her sadistic point of view. "Yes," I said, "I'd like to get this cheque cashed, please."

"Do you have an account here?" she said, looking off somewhere in the distance, probably fantasizing about being a model for *Victoria's Secret*.

"Yes, I do." I pulled out my book and handed her the cheque.

She looked at it as though I'd just handed her a steaming turd. She could barely stand to pick it up; it was as if she was afraid she'd catch something. She stared at it as though it was written partly in Greek and partly in Gaelic.

I waited, knowing what was coming. You can tell.

She was enjoying it; boy, was she enjoying it.

"I'm sorry, sir, but we can't cash this."

"Why not?" I ask.

"Do you have any money in your account?"

What an awful question. I hate that question. Of course I didn't have any money in my fucking account. Did I look like I had any money in my fucking account? Besides, I wouldn't have been trying to cash a cheque if I did.

I decided to be honest. She was bound to find out anyway. "No, I don't."

"Well, then, I'm sorry."

"What's the problem?" I said. "It's a business cheque."

"Is it?" she said and picked up the steaming turd by the corner again.

"Yes," I said.

"Well, it may be a business cheque, but it doesn't have a business signature."

I didn't know what the fuck she was talking about. "What the hell do you mean by that?"

"Excuse me, sir, but could you not get angry, please?"

Boy, do I hate it when people ask me not to get angry. I'll get angry anytime I want to, thank you, especially when you tell me *not* to.

"What's wrong with the signature?" I said. I was still hoping for justice, I swear to God I don't know why.

"Well, this cheque . . ." she said, still holding it by the corner and staring up at the fucking ceiling, looking for her brain, "this cheque is signed by a person."

"Signed by a person?"

"Yes, sir."

"So?"

"So," she looked at me as if I'd only recently, and sadly, graduated from some community college for the mentally challenged, "it has to be signed by a machine. Or else it is not a business cheque."

"Well, what the fuck are you talking about? Since when is a machine better than a person?" I said. I thought this was an incredibly persuasive argument.

Miss Wong was not, however, impressed by my philosophical musing. She rang a buzzer.

"Excuse me." I tapped on the window. "Excuse me. . . ."

Miss Wong gazed off into another room, where, I guessed, her incredibly sexy lover was undressing her with his eyes or something. She rang the buzzer again. Finally, Mr. Presser, a very annoying little faggot clerk, came marching up to her.

"Yes, Miss Kazan?" he said. "What seems to be the problem?"

Oh, that was it. Her name wasn't Wong. She was married to Elia Kazan. It made sense. Elia Kazan was the Hollywood director creep who ratted on all those communists and then got an Academy Award, a special one, for everything he'd done for the "community." It made perfect sense that she'd be married to him.

"Could you ask this man to leave? He just swore at me." And she looked off at one of the pastoral landscapes on the walls as though she was really hoping to get buggered by some sheep.

Natty little Mr. Presser turned to me. "I'm sorry, sir, you'll have to leave."

I could tell he had no idea I was a faggot. He just thought I was a rubby. Well, I'd get him some day. I'd meet him in an alley, fuck the living daylights out of him, and give him AIDS — and he'd love the whole experience, the fruity little fart. But unfortunately I couldn't do it *right then* because he was protected by the bars and the glass. Suddenly, the security measures seemed to be sensible.

I yelled into the teller's window, "Fuck you, you cunt!"

After that, I made sure to go to that lovely little branch every other day for two weeks. I'd stand in line with everybody else, and it was such a lousy little branch that no one would notice. Finally, when it was my turn to go to the window, I'd walk right over to Miss Kazan, whether she was my teller or not, and yell, "Fuck you, you cunt!" Even calm, slick Miss Kazan had the shakes after a couple of weeks. Eventually, they watched for me and wouldn't let me into the bank. They also got this cop to make me admit that I'd done wrong to Miss Kazan and that I was sorry and wouldn't do it again.

In court, this incident with the cop was supposed to prove that

I knew right from wrong. But, hey, the cop had had me cornered; I would have said anything to get rid of him! They were all at the trial. Miss Kazan and Mr. Presser, the cop, and even the bouncer — I mean security guard. The prosecution made a big deal of how planned my strategic terrorizing of Miss Kazan was and said it proved I certainly wasn't crazy — just calculating and evil.

I thought the matter was still pretty much open for discussion.

All About Cindy Lou

I guess I'd better tell you how I found out about the private lives of all the jurors. I know I go a bit overboard telling you about them. But I don't want this to be one of those stories where you ask, "How the fuck did he know what colour of toenail polish she was wearing?" Or, "How did he know whether or not that guy used to shove three fingers up his ass during masturbation?" It's like all those autobiographers who tell you their life stories and then say, "Oh, yes, back in 1922 Cyril said to me, 'I think your taste in shoes is retrograde in the extreme, you swashbuckling dude!'" Now, first of all, we all know nobody used the word *dude* in 1922. But more to the point, how the fuck did old Clive remember *what* Cyril said to him and exactly *how* he said it? So, whether you're reading this or somebody is reading it to you (I don't know, you could be blind or something), I want you to know that, when it comes to most of these stories about the jurors, I eventually got the details from Miss Cindy Lou. She has a lot of time on her hands being an unattractive spinster and everything. I *have* embellished a bit. Because, for some reason, I think I can imagine what's going on in their little juror brains.

I don't know, maybe I am crazy.

Anyway, this is supposed to be about Cindy Lou.

Now, I'm going to say what I'm going to say because I'm a

homosexual. I am a homosexual, you know, however much I hate many homosexuals — and myself.

As a fag, I've never had much use for women. Not like straight men, who still suck up to them so they can get some tail. No, to me women are just boring — unless they're not. You know what I mean? Some women are pretty fascinating. The dirty ones, the foul-mouthed ones, the ones who happen to be fucking smart. But these types of women happen to be few and far between.

So, when I started to get these letters from Cindy Lou, I laughed. I laughed out loud. What a fucking stupid cunt she was. Really. She epitomized everything I hate about women. I could tell just from reading her letters that she never masturbated. That she had no relationship with her fat, ugly body. And that she probably collected little glass figurines like Laura in *The Glass Menagerie.* Really, from what she wrote in her letters, it sounded like all she was missing was *the limp.*

A sexless victim, that's Miss Cindy Lou.

Now, why she was writing these letters, I don't know. Actually, I guess I do. I think that she was so fucking sex starved, so fucking lonely (because, stupid as she was, she was a lot smarter than the half-wits in this one-horse town), that she had to make contact with somebody. If you knew what the people in this town are like — just staring at the jury was enough to make me puke — you'd understand what drove her to write to me. I mean, she'd obviously read a book or two.

It's true: a little learning is a dangerous thing.

I think that, because she pretty well believed she was the world's biggest, ugliest misfit, when she heard about me she thought, "Here's a bigger misfit. Fatter and uglier than I am. Maybe he's my true love."

Imagine.

I also think that it had to do with my paintings. I made the mistake of telling her about my so-called art. Cindy Lou likes to think of herself as a cultured person, and I even sent her a photo of one of my paintings, ripped out of the only book ever written about my work. Oh, my God, she was impressed.

I feel like I should say something about my paintings even though I hate talking about them. I mean, they are what they are. Talking about them is stupid.

Anyway, I made some money for a while because I was a cheap imitation Rothko. You know how Rothko always paints a huge dark square blob of brown in the middle of a white canvas? I don't know if you've ever seen a Rothko for real, but they are pretty fucking impressive. In a book, they just look geometric, maybe a bit fuzzy, but not inspiring. Up close, in a gallery, they're amazing. Like giant doorways. It's as if you could walk into them and enter another world.

The thing is, I'm not into that "other world" shit. So it occurred to me to paint my own Rothkos, only different. I made big dark circles and "hung" them on the floor. Instead of paintings that give you hope, ones that make you feel you are going fly away into another universe, mine were more likely to make you feel you were going to fall. Into a big old shitty hole. It seemed more attuned to my sensibility to paint like that. I mean, I'm not spiritual, right?

So for a while I made a lot of money off these shit-hole paintings. It's all gone now, but if I want to impress people (like Aaron or Cindy Lou) I just rip a page out of that book and send it to them. It usually works. I haven't got many picture pages left, though, and it's the last copy. It's been out of print for a long time.

These days I don't paint as much. Killing people takes up a lot of time. Besides, painting is irrelevant. I'd make videos if I could afford the technology.

Now, why, you might ask, would I court an overweight, small-town spinster like Cindy Lou?

At first, I got a kick out of her stupid letters. That's why I've put some of them in here. They're pretty funny.

And when I got to Kasper and she wanted to visit me, an idea began to form: maybe she could help me out. Maybe it would be good to have a small-town ally.

Then I got the idea for her to tell me about the jurors, and then I got, well, some other ideas.

The Private Lives of Jurors 2 and 3

I put them together because I think they're both very sad.

And you might say to yourself, "Who's Kasper to call someone sad? He's either crazy or evil. And he's certainly ugly. He killed his only chance at happiness — Aaron. So where does he get off judging anyone?"

I judge because we all do, because that's the way we're made.

It makes me feel better, okay?

When I think of Minda Jenkins and Sam Waterhouse, I wonder what it would be like to be inside their brains. Why? Because I think their thoughts and vision are particularly constricted. What would it be like to go through life like that? With their very limited viewpoints? It's like Minda and Sam are in a trance, that the trance *is* their life.

Sam lives in a very small house just outside downtown Kasper, on the way to Bessemer Bend. The house is very small. Almost a miniature. He's lived there all his life. He's never been married, and he has two dogs. The dogs are Sam's pride and joy.

Sam worked for Standard Oil for many years and for the Mace factory after Standard Oil closed down. Then he retired. He has a good pension. Everyday he sits outside his house with his two dogs and watches people go by.

Sam has never had much of a sex life. No girlfriends. It just never happened. He prefers to play cards with other men — no, he's not a fag. He goes to church on Sunday (Baptist), and he doesn't question much of anything. When people ask Sam how he's doing, he says, "Fine." He has very pink skin and teeth that are a bit too big for his mouth and large, bulging, doglike eyes. Sam seems to be really sweet, and no one wonders if he's truly happy.

What's happiness? What's contentment?

Sam's fine.

During the trial, Sam stared at me with a sweet, even gaze. I could never tell what he was thinking.

Actually, he wasn't thinking at all.

Sam was one of the more stubborn jurors. His stubbornness was quiet and well meaning. Whenever he was asked to speak about me — about my life and crimes — he'd say, "Well, I just don't think he's a good man. He seems like a bad man."

"How do you know?" the other jurors would ask, looking for a fresh take on the evidence.

"I've got a feeling he's bad, that's all."

A *feeling*.

There was nothing anyone could do. Sam wasn't being an asshole intentionally. No, he was being, well, Sam. The man's IQ is low, but he's not retarded. He just lives in a simple world. Of dogs and memories. Of oil and Mace.

Next to him, in the back row, sat Minda Jenkins. I was sure that the filthy testimony troubled her and that she was coming to her judgement aurally. How did I know this?

Minda is blind.

Not many people are aware of this, but most blind people don't live in a world of total blackness. Most have vision that's partially impaired. Minda can see colours and shapes sometimes. But that's about all. She has very thick glasses with black frames, but usually they aren't much help at all.

Her life is very sad. She's never been able to see much, but as a girl, with those coke-bottle glasses, she could almost make out expressions.

In her late twenties, Minda found a nice man to marry; he worked as a cowhand on one of the ranches outside Kasper. They were happy for about fifteen years. Had two boys. One became a member of a White Power organization and tattooed a swastika on his arm. He still lives in Kasper and visits her sometimes. The other boy moved to New York City. She's never heard from him again.

The most important incident in Minda's life was her divorce. Her husband knew her sight was getting worse, but as the darkness or, more accurately, fogginess started to descend his interest in her decreased. The boys had grown up and left the house. When he left, Minda was alone and blind.

Her husband left her for a younger woman. She wasn't blind. They had a passionate affair. Leather and whips and chains — the whole bit.

Minda's life, severely limited by her poor vision, centred on visits with her lady friends from church and the monthly visits of her racist son.

The good thing about her blindness? Minda could never really make out the swastika.

"What is that, dear? A tattoo?"

"I told you, Mom. It's a swastika."

"Oh, don't fool your old mother, dear."

Cindy Lou told me that everyone in town knew the son was a Nazi, everyone except for blind old Minda.

Minda was offended, at times nauseated, by the trial. She was a deeply religious, Christian woman. But she did her civic duty. I felt very sad when I saw her squinting without seeing me, squinting through thick, useless glasses. She still *tried* to see. Could never shake the habit.

I'm sure you find it pitiful that I, a murderer, put myself above these people. But murderers have feelings too, especially for those less fortunate.

One guy limited by his intelligence, one gal by her vision. What would it be like to really get inside their heads?

It seems to me that Minda has never really seen anything properly, she probably doesn't miss what she's never known. And since Sam never thinks about anything, how can he yearn?

I happen to be educated enough to know that the verses of Ossian say "Why awaken me o breath of spring? Because the world is only sorrow."

Would you rather be Sam, Minda, or me?

Would you rather be a man who never dreams anything? Or a woman who dreamed a very limited dream once, for a moment, but will never dream again? Or a man who always dreams — but dreams of murder?

I'll let you be the judge.

My Trial

Robbie the Leather Guy was by far the most ridiculous witness called. In some ways, The Street Girl was worse because she was so dippy, but Robbie was so much more pretentious. I see him as the sort of ultimate flower of the gay-liberation movement. And, as Oscar Wilde said, "I'm sure you know what that unfortunate movement led to. . . ." Well, it led to Robbie Boxer.

I don't know if you know much about gay politics of the 1970s, before AIDS started killing people and consequently shutting them up. But it was a time when gay men started to look, act, and talk like "men." Before that, being gay was all about being effeminate and thin and boylike. Suddenly, in the late 1970s, masculinity was the thing. There was this artist, "Tom of Finland," who was producing these great drawings of guys doing each other — on ranches, in workboots, and in leather. He said he was giving gay men the "right" to be masculine, and sure enough it caught on. A lot of guys started wearing workboots and taking pride in their leather and cowboy hats.

Now, let's get something straight. I've got nothing against anybody being masculine. That's fine with me. I'm pretty masculine myself, actually. But when people make a fucking fetish out of it? That's another thing. I hate ultramasculine fags as much as I hate the ultrafeminine ones. Basically, yeah, I hate everybody.

Anyway, a certain type of fag was born in the late 1970s and early 1980s. This type of guy thinks that all fags should be masculine, that masculine is somehow better than feminine. Most of these fags are deluded.

See, they actually think they're butch. It's the classic gay cliché: some prissy little queen starts believing that leather makes him a real guy above everybody else. Robbie was a perfect example of this.

I need to describe him physically, it's important. He was grotesque and ugly. Skinny and tall. Not skinny in a nice way, skinny in a pasty, slightly flabby, hairy way. His brown hair was very curly (which is bad enough in my books), but he was so proud of it that he had it cut in a huge Afro. The problem being, of course, he wasn't black. So, on the one hand, he's this leather guy who thinks he's masculine; on the other hand, he's got this silly Afro he's so proud of, fucking up the image — not to mention how skinny and femmy he is. Never mind, Afro or no Afro, femmy or not femmy — Robbie saw himself as the ultimate emissary of the leather community. He called himself "a person *of* leather." All I could think about, when Robbie talked like this, was a whole bunch of leather dolls lined up on a shelf at a fair, with people throwing rocks at them. Every time there was a "leather event," Robbie would preside, judging all the contests and stuff.

Who's got the biggest "manballs"? Who's got the hairiest ass? Who can sit on a bowling pin and then lift it in the air with his asshole? Edifying, soul-improving contests like that.

One day he wrote a letter to the editor of the local gay rag saying that he was offended when drag queens came into leather bars.

"There I am," Robbie wrote, "cruising some hot guy in leather. A dark burly man — a real man — dripping with sweat and smelling of pre-cum. . . ."

Oh, *please.*

"And *then* a nelly girlfriend comes into the bar in drag. Well, there goes my hard-on! Bye bye!"

Jesus. As if anybody ever cared whether Robbie had a hard-on or not.

So he was sort of on a campaign to keep the bars clear of drag queens. Especially the leather bars. They were "masculine" territory.

Well, I never used to think much about all this political junk. I'd go to a bar — not thinking much about what I draped over my ugly, fat, smelly carcass — with the intention of having some fun and maybe infecting a few dumb faggots. And one summer, when it was really hot and I was really lazy, I decided to wear a long skirt made out of camouflage material instead of pants. Call me crazy. Anyway, I lived in a building filled with sad drag queens, so I was sure that nobody *there* would bat an eye.

I looked pretty good in a skirt. And my big hairy belly hung over the edge, in case anyone was interested in that kind of gross thing. It was cool *and* practical.

I went to a local bar looking for victims, and it happened to be a leather place. Sure enough, after fifteen minutes of sipping my drink, old Robbie came scurrying up to me, his Afro quivering, all in a flap.

"I'm sorry," he said, "we don't allow drag in this bar."

"The doorman let me in," I said, ignoring him.

"He probably thought you were wearing camouflage pants."

"Yeah, too bad, I'm not."

"I'm sorry, but you'll have to leave."

"I'm not going to leave."

"You have to."

"I'm not."

This went on for a while, with Robbie threatening to call a couple of his more "masculine" leather friends over, since he certainly wasn't big enough to throw me out. Then it got to the point where he was just yabbering on and on about how important it was to have a space for "real men" to hang out. I just couldn't stand it anymore. I just couldn't stand hearing this silly pansy, who thought he was a real man, flap his ugly — probably AIDS-infected — gums at me. So I poured my beer over his head. It was an impulse, and it was the right one. It felt very good. Robbie looked funny dripping with beer. Kinda like a wet weasel in leather. All I could think about was how long it would take him to get the stickiness out of his Afro.

Robbie didn't do anything. What could he do? He was too "masculine" to have a hissy fit and too much of a wimp to punch me out. So he marched off in a fury. No one else did anything. Nobody tried to kick me out. I don't think anybody really gave a fuck if a big ugly guy like me wanted to wear a skirt. I mean, I wasn't acting the part of a fucked-up drag diva, like Whiny Betty, I was just trying to give the dumb fags easy access on a hot night.

But that wasn't the end of it. And that's why all of this became "relevant" to the prosecution's case.

After that night, Robbie sent me a whole bunch of e-mails. I don't know how he got my address, but he's an e-mail queen, and he cruises leather chatrooms. In his e-mails, he chewed me out for having lost my temper. He said I should learn to control my "irrational rages."

I made the mistake of e-mailing him back and making it very clear that I hadn't been in a rage. "You deserved to have a bottle of beer poured over your head, Robbie," I wrote. "It was not an irrational rage. It was a carefully planned and considered decision. I intended to get your stupid, ugly Afro sticky. I don't have rages, Robbie. I only make rational decisions."

Boy, that was a mistake. The prosecution played these words for all they were worth.

Here's some advice. If you ever plan on murdering someone and copping a plea of craziness, don't go around explaining your actions to people. Especially in e-mails. It will get you into trouble, I guarantee it.

More About Cindy Lou

I want to tell you about meeting Cindy Lou in person. It was the one and only time, and, boy, was it traumatic.

For both of us.

I didn't think it would have such an effect. Like I said, to me she was just a stupid cunt, falling in love with me via snail mail. I didn't care about her. But I figured that, if we met, I could milk her for juror information and get a few books. So she came to the prison (there's only one prison in Kasper) and brought me things.

All the stuff she'd told me about the June Bug Epidemic and The Phantom Anesthetist really interested me at the time. I wasn't sure why, but I wanted to read more. Mainly, I was just very bored.

Also, I wanted to read the book by Anita Bryant. Cindy Lou was very hepped up on the idea that a lot of my views were the same as hers. That we both hate homosexuals a lot. I tried to explain to her that I didn't hate all homosexuals, just the stupid ones (admittedly, there are a lot of stupid ones), but she insisted that I had a lot in common with Bryant, so just to solve the argument I wanted to read *The Anita Bryant Story: The Survival of the Nation's Families and the Threat of Militant Homosexuality*.

Of course, Cindy Lou insisted on bringing her two other favourite books: *The Fountainhead* and the Bible.

I'll admit, when she came in, I was shocked by her appearance. She was so ugly and pitiful that I thought the only way I could possibly keep from laughing was to compliment her excessively. Which I did.

She really bought it.

It's hard to describe Cindy Lou. The most dramatic ugly thing about her is that her hair is just so flat and greasy. Why doesn't she just wash it? But she *must* wash it. She *must* know about human hygiene. I guess her hair is just *that way*. I mean, she claims to have lifeless hair. But don't they have lots of expensive hair-care products for that? Maybe not in Wyoming. It didn't help that she wore these gold kitten berets, which made it flatter. And then there's her weight. It isn't just that she's fat — I've seen fat girls who don't look so bad. It's that she has no breasts at all and a gigantic stomach. Her body is a lot like mine, actually. Even her face is pudgy. And red. And sort of squashed.

Cindy Lou is incredibly unattractive, almost deformed.

In a way, it was like looking in a mirror.

That's something that I never told you. I never look in mirrors.

It's probably the strangest thing about me. Maybe it has to do with being so ugly, maybe it has to do with being a killer, I don't know. To me, all mirrors distort. They just don't tell the truth. My proof? Well, just have a look in a mirror sometime, then go back five minutes later and look again. I guarantee that you won't look the same. Mirrors are as untrustworthy as photographs. One minute you catch a glimpse of yourself on a shiny toaster, and you look maybe half okay. The next minute you pass a reflective shop window, and you look like Shelly Winters crawling out from the *Poseidon* one last time.

So, anyway, I just don't look in mirrors. But when Cindy Lou walked into my cell, I was suddenly given the only true mirror there was. Looking at somebody as ugly as me was very unsettling.

Anyway, she gave me the books right away, and she was very nice. But all she ever did was ask me about her looks. You see, she had a new hairdo that day.

"How do I look with my hair like this?" she must have said almost twenty-five times in different ways. "Do you think it flatters my face? . . . Do you think it's too young a cut for me? . . . Do you think it accents my negative points?"

She went on and on. It was hard to make her happy — and I did want to make her happy because I was beginning to think that her info about the jurors would be useful. And that the books might keep me from going crazy.

But then she started to piss me off. Which was a bad thing. Very bad. I was tired of telling her how good she looked. And I was lying.

So I stopped. You know, it struck me that she was in a kind of self-image trance. I'm not saying that Cindy Lou could have done something more with what God gave her. Honestly, God gave that girl very little. But, you know, there are some really ugly people in this world who believe that they're beautiful. They really do. *And that helps.* And it's like Cindy Lou was in this ugly trance, so no matter what I said she didn't believe me. I mean, she pretended to believe me, but I knew she didn't. And at one point, I thought it didn't really matter what I said. She wasn't going to believe she's a hot babe, so why not just tell her off?

I was really annoyed, not thinking rationally.

Anyway, finally I said, "I think your hair hides any hint of fatness."

Oh, my God. I said the F-word. It was not the right word to use *at all.* She, of course, was allowed to use the word *fat* about herself; when I used it, she lost her noodle. I should have known better.

She gradually went nuts. "What do you mean fat? Are you saying I'm fat?"

"No, I'm not saying you're fat."

"But you used the word *fat.*"

"No, I used the word *fatness.*"

"But *fatness* has the word *fat* in it."

She had me there.

I guess, ultimately, I was pretty unkind. I didn't mean to be. I think it happened because she was so neurotic, and because I don't like looking in a mirror, and because Cindy Lou was the closest thing to a mirror I had experienced since I stopped looking in mirrors.

When she stomped out, I could tell she was pissed off. Cindy Lou was committed to staying in her little ugly trance, and there was nothing I could do to snap her out of it. In fact, I'd made it worse.

That whole battle had some good and some bad consequences.

It depends on how you look at it.

Jurors 4–7: Be Very Afraid

I've always had this theory about people and trances. I think it's interesting but may require some proof.

It's hard to explain because one of the big problems is that, when you're in a trance, you don't know you're in it. The only way you really know is when you wake up. Then you can say, "Oh, hey, I was in a trance."

A lot like consciousness, or what we know of it, my theory is Platonic. That is, here we are, each in our own little consciousness. And we think that we know others, and we think that we think like they think, perceive like they perceive, because we're all human, right? But we can never get inside somebody's head to see how that person thinks, because then we'd no longer be separate beings. So we're condemned to guess what everyone's headspace is. We're given little signals, which are like Plato's cave shadows. And we think we can guess, from the flickering there, what's going on, but we'll never really know.

That's what happened with Cindy Lou. I had no way of knowing how severe her trance was. So severe that I couldn't even say the word *fat* — the word that most came to mind when looking at her — in her presence.

My theory is that everybody is in his or her own little trance. It's very hard for us to get together and commiserate, though. Still, I think that most of our trances can be traced to one thing and one thing alone: fear.

Most of us are afraid. Now, let's face it, there's a lot to fear. There are unknowns such as death, and there's pain and suffering. There's loneliness and ridicule and ugliness and defeat. And that's just the tip of the iceberg. Mostly, I think that our parents, because of all the ugliness in the world or something (sorry, I can't explain it all), use fear to discipline us. Parents won't just say, "Don't touch the burner, Johnny, you'll burn your hand." They say, "Stop it, Johnny, stop! You'll burn in hell, you dirty bad boy, if you ever do that again." The result? Terror. We walk around in a fear trance.

There were four jurors — all sat in the back row — who were, as far as I was concerned, terrified. I used to stare at them. Maybe that's what terrified them? No, I don't think so. As far as I could tell, they were just plain terrified. Bunnies in headlights. You could see it in their eyes. Cindy Lou gave me the details.

Taffy Longstreet, Leopold Waddle, John Miller, and Annie Plather.

Annie was my favourite. She had glossy, straight, dark, Monica Lewinsky hair combed flat to her head. She was possessed of a marvellous bosom from which she couldn't, no matter how hard she tried, divert men's attention. Cindy Lou, not having any tits, went on and on about Annie's. Annie was a housewife, and her husband was a very successful computer software salesman. She had two darling children, both boys.

What I liked about Annie was that she was afraid of being found out. On the surface, she was pleasant, even-tempered, and intelligent. No real quirks as far as most people could tell. Deep down, though, she was a dominatrix.

Cindy Lou told me all about it, with utmost disgust, of course. And she didn't use the word *dominatrix*. But I knew exactly what she was talking about. I could see it in Annie's eyes.

Annie discovered her desire for dominance at an early age while playing with the neighbourhood boys and girls. She played a game called Master and Slave. Annie was the master, and all the other little kids were tied up. She'd walk around the room and hit them with a cat-o'-nine-tails. The whipping didn't hurt much, and Annie's punishing words were sexy. And, yeah, the kids were naked.

Nothing much came of the whipping sessions. But Annie never forgot them. I'm sure that long after she married Fred Plather they became her tiny, private obsession. She didn't want to become a hooker or anything, she just wanted to slap some people around now and then.

Annie was taught by her church and family, of course, that these were the impulses of a whore. Everybody in Kasper agreed. So Annie lived in fear of her own impulses and of her own hand. I know that sometimes her hand must have gotten out of control. I'll bet that, when her husband was making love to her, she just wanted to lift her hand to his ample buttocks and slap away. She knew that such an act would have horrified Fred and brought her to instant orgasm. She also knew what kind of women were obsessed with orgasms.

So Annie kept her impulses under control, but there was one time that Cindy Lou told me about. It almost became a big scandal. Annie punished her eleven-year-old son a little too severely and bruised his behind so badly that the child bled (the nurse at school discovered it). The boy, after all, had been *particularly bad*.

John Miller's terror was of another order. John had no passions, absolutely none. It was evident just from looking at him. For years, he'd worked as a bank accountant. As a young man, he'd worked for his father's real estate business.

John had always lived in the shadow of his brother, Buck. Buck was older, and his mother and father always called him "Sonny." What was John if Buck was Sonny? John was just, well, John.

He went to war in Korea, and when he came back it was time to marry a Kasper girl, Sue Darlington. Sue was pretty, and John almost believed he might feel passionately about her. But she quickly divorced him and took the kids. She didn't come right out and say it, but she thought John was unbearably boring.

Out of desperation and loneliness, John then married a sweet, twenty-three-year-old thing named Adelaide. She was even prettier than Sue, but Adelaide was also pregnant with someone else's child. She was using John. Bad luck.

Cindy Lou told me all the gossip — and that Buck took John aside and recommended he marry an older woman (she was thirty-eight, closer to John's age) named Abigail. She was a librarian, not very attractive, and not at all pregnant. She was perfect. Everyone agreed.

The only problem was that John didn't care about anything. He didn't care about his job at the bank or his marriage to the homely Abigail. There wasn't anything overtly wrong with his life, there just didn't seem to be a reason for living. I'm sure this emptiness plagued him until he died.

It made him very human and kind of sweet.

Taffy Longstreet was just like her name. Small, sharp, and cute as a button. She couldn't help but wear bright colours all the time. Taffy would wear yellow-and-blue, or orange-and-purple, dresses with matching shoes and complementary stockings. Her blonde hair was bobbed short but swung casually about her lovely face. After high school, she became a registered nurse, but there was only one problem.

She hated the human body.

She also, of course, hated sex.

For Taffy, anatomy classes were torture. So was gym, probably, and so were dates. She probably didn't want to date but knew she had to.

One time she went out with an engineering student from Laramie.

Blake, the student, was nice enough. He promised not to touch her. She always made boys promise not to touch her on the first date — little did they know that they weren't to touch her *ever*. Taffy quite enjoyed the movie until Blake offered her popcorn. She probably said, "Sure, Blake, thanks!" When she reached down into the box, what did she find there? Well, Blake — who'd recently seen the hit movie *Diner* with his engineering friends — had placed the cylindrical popcorn box over his cock and balls. His cock wasn't that large, even when engorged, and she bypassed it and found her hand pressing against his warm and fuzzy scrotum.

Like all girls in Kasper, Taffy had heard tell of scrotums and had always been upset merely by the *idea* of them.

She shrieked and ran out of the theatre and had to be taken to the hospital in an ambulance.

Just imagine what it was like for sex-hating little Taffy. Something about touching the hairy, wrinkly sac, tight and swollen with desire, tweaked her deepest fears.

She underwent sedation and therapy and didn't recover for weeks.

Kasperians thought it was terrible but found her extreme reaction a little odd. "After all," many said, "you know those engineers!"

Her fear of the human body made it difficult for her later in life. Taffy never got a job as a nurse, and instead she became a doctor's receptionist. She was cheerful and pretty, and it was the perfect job for her, though she did have to avoid the doctor's anatomy charts. Eventually, she knew that she *had* to marry, and she found Ken Longstreet, who was, thankfully, almost as afraid of the physical side of marriage as she was. She managed to get impregnated once.

I can imagine her prodding him in the dark, "Be quick, Kenny! Oh, please, dear God — be quick!" It was a *nightmare*, but she wasn't going to deny herself the joys of motherhood.

Praise the Lord, it was a little girl — so Taffy would never have to wash a scrotum! Kenny had a good job in the insurance business, so they had a nanny who washed the child anyway.

Taffy found the world difficult. It was always, it seemed, getting more and more physical. And the images on television, well, she just couldn't watch TV or movies. And wouldn't allow Erica, her daughter, to watch them either.

Taffy was more afraid than usual in the courtroom, I could tell. The way she looked at me? Mortal terror. Now and then, as she watched me, her pale little hand would move to cover her horrified mouth. I fantasized, because I have a very round, very bald cranium, that as she stared my head morphed, slowly and inexplicably, into a gigantic, wrinkly scrotum.

Leopold Waddle was the final bundle of terror. I remember his pale, taut skin and that he had the eyes of a frightened child. Beneath his neck, however, was the wild, unruly chest hair of a very adult man.

As a child, Leopold was muscular and athletic, and he'd once attended a private school in Colorado. The experience never left him. He loved the rigid discipline. The marching, the time that was so carefully divided into bits and accounted for. He loved being told what to do. He was terrified of ever having to think or act for himself.

Leopold longed for a military career, but his father and mother, who'd made millions from Standard Oil, refused to allow him to become a common soldier. The dilemma was that along with his love of coercion, punishment, and order he lacked the backbone to stand up to them. So he went to the high-level, high-paying job his father found for him at the Mace factory and never left it.

Leopold married and had one boy, whom Leopold enjoyed

dressing for a while in sailor suits. Until people *talked*.

His pride and joy, though, was the collection of toy soldiers he'd play with endlessly, late into the night. He had equally extensive collections of both tin soldiers and the more dangerous, but antique and valuable, lead ones. On her one visit to Leopold's house, Cindy Lou had been treated to a guided tour.

Leopold started a collection of GI Joes ostensibly as gifts for his son. But Rory wasn't interested in dolls; the boy was very mechanical.

Occasionally, Leopold's wife, an Amway salesperson, would go away on business. It's *my* theory that Leopold found taking a GI Joe to bed with him led to violent masturbatory orgasms, much more intense than those he'd had with his wife. Rory was quite masculine and unsexual.

Now and then, after playing with his tin or lead soldiers, Leopold would pack away his things in a "kit" bag he'd saved from school and march off into the night. He'd get onto the bus for Lander — the state capital — where there was an army enlistment office. But he'd always lose his nerve and get off before Hell's Half Acre — there was a rest stop at Powder River — and call Al's Cab and head home, defeated. I'm sure that he was secretly afraid he'd die without ever marching "in step" again.

Cindy Lou got these details from Rory. Luckily, she kept her mouth shut — Leopold was terrified that someone would find out.

While sitting at the defence desk, I'd look to Leopold, John, Annie, and Taffy and feel sorry for them because they were so afraid. But I'd also feel sorry for myself; I knew that for them I was a sudden, crash course in existentialism. I had, ultimately, made *choices*. Even choosing to kill is, after all, a choice.

They were so paralysed by fear that they couldn't *act*. Sure, they got married, had jobs, the usual — in our culture, that's what you have to do. But none of them could imagine the choices I'd made, such dangerous and irrational ones.

And I know that Taffy, for one, just wanted that big wrinkly scrotum — my head — dead and buried.

The sooner the better.

My Trial

The turning point of my case?

Well, at first I didn't take the trial too seriously. I figured the worst that could happen was they'd put me in an insane asylum. I mean, nobody *enjoys* infecting people with AIDS unless he's insane, right? And they'd have to prove beyond the shadow of a doubt that I had infected all these little slutbags, right? And even sweet little Aaron was a slut from hell.

As the trial continued, I realized that it wasn't like this at all. It wasn't about medical evidence or science or insanity or madness. It was about me, ugly old me. It was about me sitting there looking like an unrepentant Hunchback of Notre Dame and Aaron sitting there looking like an angel. It was about them imagining us having sex together. It was about the horror. To the jury, we were the heart of darkness. Or, rather, I was. Because for sure the trial was about the idea that I must have seduced Aaron into my dark ways. I knew they were thinking, "It's unfortunate that this pretty boy has to be a homosexual: he'd probably be okay if he hadn't somehow come in contact with that monster who infected him." They thought that Aaron was innocent because he was pale and beautiful and weak and had kind eyes.

God, I'm so jealous sometimes of what beautiful people get away with. They say that they get better marks in school and that their basic success rate in life is much higher than it is for ugly people like me. I believe it.

Did Aaron's mother and father know that Aaron had got scabby knees from blowing all those guys in Italy? Did they know he was into scuz? Did they know he used to lick the jam from between my toes? Oh, no, he was too sweet and pretty and fragile for that.

I wanted to be the one to tell them, but I knew it wouldn't do much good. It was a jury of frightened, religious, small-town nuts.

But would it have been any different in New York City? I don't think so. Beauty is beauty, and ugliness is ugliness. And since ugliness is evil, beauty must be good and clean.

So, for a time, I behaved irresponsibly, acting crazy because I thought it would get me committed. I figured that I belonged in an asylum, that it was probably where I'd be happiest. After all, I'd be able to sit around and masturbate and take drugs all day, right? And inevitably there'd be some gay nutbars in there with me. Trying to prove myself insane, I'm pretty sure I ended up looking like a total idiot. For instance, some days I would stare at Aaron and then stare at the jury — and then make a motion of my hand that looked a bit like I was jerking off. No, it wasn't too blatant, I didn't want to get kicked out of the courtroom. It was just enough to make me look like an insane wanker. On other occasions, I flirted with the jury. Especially the women. That really freaked them out.

But as time went by, I realized what a farce the trial had become, and I gave up. I started thinking that, if they believed I was making fun of the whole process, then I might end up in jail for life.

I know you think I don't give a shit about myself. That's true; I don't. It's also true that I'm an evil killer and that I deserve everything I get.

But day after day, there were all these people constantly affirming that I was perfectly sane and evil. So, yeah, I began to dread rotting away in a Wyoming jail, because I was pretty sure they wouldn't fry me. If only Aaron had been a resident of Texas, where death row is a state of mind.

So, okay, I got angry. The more witnesses they brought in, and the more I stared at the dumb jury, the more I thought: "I don't deserve to be hounded to death just because I'm ugly and evil, at least I'm not like the rest of the hypocritical world!" Then I got this idea that I might have a chance of getting off *as a sane person*.

It all had to do with Miss Cindy Lou Williams.

I began to mull over my trance theory. About people being trapped in their own consciousnesses, unable to get out. And I began to think about how Cindy Lou was trapped in her ugly trance, something that no pixie haircut could ever save her from. And then I began to think about Anita Bryant and some of the pamphlets about hysteria that Cindy Lou had brought me.

"Maybe," I thought, "we're all in some kind of trance. Even me."

And I know it sounds crazy. But suddenly I began to connect the so-called AIDS epidemic and the June Bug Epidemic and The Phantom Anesthetist of Altoona. Because, after all, if I could prove that AIDS wasn't real, then they'd have to acknowledge that I couldn't have killed anybody with it. If it was all inside people's heads, then I couldn't be a murderer. I mean, the whole trial was ludicrous anyway. Nobody ever brought in a doctor to talk about my condition or the conditions of the people, including Aaron, who claimed to have been infected by me. So, if I could go all medical on them, maybe I could save my life.

The book that Cindy Lou gave me about mass hypnosis proves how real it is. People can actually *think* themselves into dying. And looking around at all the people I'd infected, I realized that most of them were psychologically sick before anything happened to their bodies.

I began working out an "AIDS is crap" defence. And, in the back of my mind, behind everything, I thought that if I could prove all this I might be able to get Aaron back.

Crazy as *that* sounds.

Because that was actually the reason for everything, wasn't it? I mean, going to the courtroom every day was having two very different effects on me: making me pissed off at all the assholes who were trashing me (even killers hate being trashed), and making me want Aaron back again.

I was very excited.

I told my lawyer that I couldn't wait to get up on the stand and speak my piece. It was what he figured would be the best defence all along. His plan was to ask me questions such as "Why did you do it?" and I was supposed to answer, "So I could kill some stupid, boring fags." Then, he figured, they'd have to find me insane. But he didn't know that I'd changed my mind.

I looked for anything that would prove my theory as they trotted out the last of the witnesses who testified I knew right from wrong.

"Fine," I thought. "Prove I'm sane. Because if I'm sane, then people will have to listen to me and take me seriously." I'd talk about my trance theories. I'd make a speech. Like that guy, Howard Roark, in the book Cindy Lou likes so much, *The Fountainhead*. Sure, it's fiction, but the whole trial seemed like fiction at that point, so why not?

They dragged out some girl I'd yelled at on the street once — she'd called me a fat, crippled faggot because I wouldn't give her money. And some ugly guy whom I wouldn't sleep with at the bathhouse once. And some clerk from a store who said I never smiled and who hated me. All of them talked about what an ugly, mean-tempered, but sane person I was. Where did they find them all? They must have put up signs in the bathhouses or something: "Did you fuck Quasimodo?"

I couldn't wait for Whiny Betty, Nick, Alphonse, and Aaron to get on the stand. I wanted to test my theory.

Seventh Prison Letter from
Cindy Lou Williams

Dear Kasper,

I don't really know where to start. When I left you the other day, I cried.

I don't say that to make you feel guilty. Not that there's any chance of that! Of course, you are entitled to your own freedom of will and action. But I was hurt by the way you treated me.

Let me remind you that you are on trial for attempting to murder a boy. The newspapers vilify you. Witness after witness has come to the stand to report that you are a cold, calculating, cruel man.

Despite all of this, I took it upon myself to write to you and then to visit you. Do you have any idea what hardship this has caused?

My mother, who has never been right since the June bug incident, needs my help and support daily. Occasionally, I have been unable to give her that help due to my letters and visit to you. I have sacrificed helping her because I wanted to give you all the support I could.

Also, I haven't been able to tell anyone about this. Only my closest friend, Maryanne, has been privy to information about my letters and prison visit. She's concerned that I'm overextending myself and doesn't really understand. But she tries to be sympathetic.

Do you know what would happen if any of my other friends or relatives found out about you? They'd think that I was crazy. My brother-in-law works for the DA's office. I have to be very careful.

So I have sacrificed closeness with family and friends to be close to you. And what do I get in return? Ridicule and humiliation, the deepest forms of hurt.

I don't know if you remember the other day — you seemed to be so cavalier in dismissing me — but you talked over and over again about my "actual fatness."

Even writing it now is difficult.

I don't think that you have any idea how much those words hurt. Are you aware of what it's like for a woman to have a weight problem? Especially a woman like me, who started out as no beauty and has limp and lifeless hair? When I was a little girl, children taunted me; I was excluded from games and parties and dates. I have waged a valiant battle of the bulge, only to be told by doctors that I am not blessed with a high metabolism. I have certainly made you aware of my sensitivity before, and yet, at the moment when you chose to say a quick and thoughtless good-bye, you hurled this most hurtful of insults at me. I can't bear it.

I am beginning to believe that you are the evil man the prosecution has been painting. I have to say that, gazing at that sweet, innocent boy, it's hard to believe he's infected with the AIDS virus. Worse, forgive me, I can't imagine that he would have had sexual intercourse with you.

There. I've said it.

I'll say more.

What happened? Are you going to tell all? Did you rape him? There can be no other reason for why he would allow himself to get close to you. You are a vile man, and I never want to see you again.

I am seriously thinking of accusing you of attempted rape. After all, you did try to rape me that day. But I forgave you. Before you hurled my fatness at me, you told me over and over again how beautiful I was, and you even caressed my face. And at one point, your hands moved toward other parts of my body.

What was all that leading to if not rape?

Now, I can forgive you nothing. Why should you be forgiven?

I hope they lock you up for the rest of your life.

Thank you, Kasper Klotz. You have taught me the meaning and importance of hate.

Sincerely,
Cindy Lou Williams

The Private Life of Juror 8

Ronald Heavyfeather was a victim. It wasn't his fault. His father was a Native American. As a child, he was urged to participate in a sport that was of his own people's invention — lacrosse.

The coach was tall and lean and blond. He loved the eleven year old with the bright dark eyes.

Ronald's mother had taught her son to clean himself thoroughly. This meant that he stayed very late and showered after playing lacrosse.

Sam Gunt, the coach, had seen other boys lather themselves. With them, it had been an indication, a signal. When he touched those boys, they were happy. They found a brief and secret ecstasy.

At first, it seemed the same was true of Ronald. Sam had no idea that the boy was devastated by the experience.

In reality, the half-Native boy enjoyed the experience but felt incredible guilt over experiencing so much pleasure. Mainly, he was tortured by the desire he felt for the tall, lean, older man.

Late at night, Ronald would listen to radio talk shows alone in his bedroom, when his mother was downstairs watching *Cagney and Lacy*. Eventually, there was a show about child molestation, and he realized that's what Sam had done to him. You see, every night Ronald would masturbate by rubbing himself against the bed, sometimes having agonizing and guilty thoughts about his experiences with his coach. One night, his father, Thomson Heavyfeather, came home late and heard passionate moans coming from his son's room. He quietly opened the door and caught his boy with the covers thrown back, his rear end moving up and down as he pressed himself passionately against the mattress.

The next day, Ronald explained the cause of his perversion to his father. Echoing the talk show, he said he'd been molested.

Ronald was twelve years old.

There was a trial much like mine. Sam was a demon, and the

whole town came out to vilify him, to catch sight of the freak.

Sam Gunt was jailed for fifteen years. Strangely, it was only for Ronald, the bright-eyed, serious, half-Native boy, that Sam had felt a stirring of real feelings. For the others, he'd felt only desire.

Ronald Heavyfeather never forgot the trial or the molestation. More importantly, he never forgot the sexual desire he felt for his molester. Countless sessions with a psychotherapist could never wipe away the pain; instead, they confirmed it and burned it into his brain. A sexless marriage to an older, quite homely woman seemed to help. Soon Ronald became an active crusader for the rights of the abused and joined a club in Cheyenne. Finally, he quit his job at a day-care centre and began to counsel victims of abuse.

Lately, Ronald had, on the recommendation of his therapist, taken to carrying a calling card. It read "Ronald Heavyfeather, Victim." Of course, the attractively designed card, printed on embossed ivory luna gloss, featured his home and e-mail addresses.

Whenever Ronald looked at Aaron, he started to cry. He couldn't look at me. All he could think about was the boy he'd been.

I'll tell you how I know all this.

I could see it in his eyes.

My Trial

I couldn't believe how neatly everything fit into my "everyone is in a trance" theory.

When they called Whiny Betty to the stand, they asked her what her job was. She smiled at the judge and said, "Female impersonator." She didn't mention the pharmacy.

Her story was lurid and pitiful. She had a Kleenex in her pocket and blew her nose obsessively, partially because she had a cold and partially because she was overcome with emotion. She explained the facts. How she'd led a blameless life of devotion to AIDS victims, raising money and caring for them. How she'd hardly ever had sex with anyone, except for the lover she'd broken up with because he'd abused her. (At least that was a new twist.) And then she talked of a terrible night, a night when she'd been in deep despair. You see, after spending a long day organizing an AIDS fundraiser for a dead friend, she'd found out about the death of *another* friend.

It truly was a holocaust, this horrible disease.

So, as a result of these tragedies, she'd become terribly depressed and broken her personal rule — and imbibed. She'd had two martinis.

And then, apparently, I'd raped her in an alley.

It was heart-wrenching.

You know, if I was still set on an insanity plea, her lies would have infuriated me. But I was beyond all that. Now Betty just fascinated me. She was an archetype: the typical fag. Caught up in the web of AIDS. I'd always known that the disease had defined Whiny Betty's life, but it had never really occurred to me exactly *how much*. She was absolutely nobody without AIDS. Of course, you see, she wasn't *really* physically ill — except for her endless sniffles. I mean, when my lawyer asked her about the details of her suffering, all she could say was "I get frequent colds!"

But what joy she experienced from being my victim. Looking at her, I wondered if she'd be able to make herself truly ill. Sick enough to die, that is. Was death necessary to make her parents truly love and value her? Even Whiny Betty's mind is a powerful thing.

It sure seemed possible to me.

Nick represented the opposite end of the same spectrum. He had bulging eyes and sunken cheeks but was tanned within an inch of his life. You could barely see the hump on his back. I could tell all the women on the jury loved him. Even Lorena Mady Kelly.

There's something about old-cheery-tubby-every-inch-a-faggot Nick that just warms the hearts of ladies everywhere. He was wearing a little leopardskin scarf and looked as though he'd just walked out of a 1950s movie. You couldn't help it, watching his precise, happy, slightly effeminate way of talking, you couldn't help thinking, "Fags are so nice." The thing that really killed me about him was that the prosecuting attorney actually had to *stop asking him questions.* They almost had to push him off the stand. He went on and on about how great it was to be HIV positive. It was ridiculous, terrible for the prosecution's case. I mean, if being HIV positive was so much fun, could I actually be guilty of attempted murder? Nick at one point *thanked* me for giving it to him. Of course, he didn't mention anything about arching his back during the act and moaning, "Give me your infected come, you big handsome man!" But still, it was as if he had.

One surprise was that Alphonse was a no-show. I guess he was dead or didn't know that I'd infected him.

The other surprise was the appearance of The Crown Prince.

He was the wackiest of all. Do you remember him? The crazy guy who used to live down the hall? Well, it turned out he just *had* to join in the AIDS fun. Remember how I told you he wasn't even HIV positive? In court, he *said* he was. They took it for granted he was telling the truth. As I said, they didn't test anyone who said I'd infected him. I guess they figured people who were willing to come forward and say they were HIV positive couldn't possibly lie. I mean, who'd pretend to have a disease that makes him a social pariah?

Anyway, suddenly The Crown Prince was HIV positive. And it was my fault, of course. He talked about our "night of passion" and how crafty I was. Because, of course, he couldn't miss the opportunity to mention his distinguished Russian ancestry. His story was that I'd brought over his favourite vodka and then seduced him by offering to dance to Rachmaninoff. Can you dance to Rachmaninoff? The prosecution had to cut Rantinovich off too. He got a little off track complaining about how badly the Russian government had treated Rachmaninoff and how they'd driven the venerable composer to defect to the West. And then about how no one has any manners anymore. Where is the charm and wit of yesteryear?

It was at this nutty point, as they were bringing up the craziest people, people whom *I would never have fucked even if I'd been paid*, that I realized this truly was *mass hysteria.* Just as The Crown Prince, like so many others, was deluded enough to believe that he was Anastasia's brother, he was susceptible to another mass delusion: that he had AIDS. He was definitely the kind of guy who might talk himself into dying. If he couldn't be the last czar, then maybe he could be a pitiful martyr.

The Private Life of Juror 9

Leah Johnson was statuesque. There was something about her . . . the way she held her head. People admired and obeyed her. She was a novelist who enjoyed no small success in Seattle.

She was married and had four children. She was working on her fifth. Her husband, Alan Whitmore, was a quiet, handsome man and a chemist.

Leah always used her maiden name.

Her early novels were "slice of life" pieces. She wrote about the black lower classes, about prostitutes and their pimps. She was able to capture the language of those whose lives had been less fortunate. It made her an enigma; her own diction was cool, relaxed, and polished. Still, there was something angry about her. A whiff of tragedy. A dash of the operatic. A soupçon of the heroic.

Her husband was pleased to worship at the feet of such an esteemed literary giantess. Only when it was time to make another baby would she let him fuck her late into the night. He knew he might not get another chance for months.

In every one of Leah's novels is a speech about the functions of the female genitals. Cindy Lou lent me one of the books. It was very difficult to read. One of Leah's prostitutes always has an abortion, a miscarriage, or a massive, dangerous period. Never all three, but always one.

The artsy, grey-haired ladies in Seattle who bought Leah's books had much sympathy for these misguided street girls with "female problems." Some of Leah's book launches were benefits for black women's organizations or the local family-planning centre.

Many commented on the gritty, often horrific street poetry of her novels. They didn't seem to notice that most of the grit and horror was linked to women's genitalia.

Another characteristic of Leah's books is that a tragedy inevitably occurs after sexual intercourse. After a night of uninterrupted sexual pleasure and release, a character experiences a gradual increase in misfortune, which leads, along with the severe "women's problems," to a premature death.

The critics in Seattle, who were mainly sexually frustrated themselves, didn't notice these subtle through-lines. They praised her novels and deified Leah as one of the nation's leading women writers.

Eventually, Leah stopped writing gritty street novels and switched to prose poems that were incomprehensible to everyone, it seemed, but the critics. And though no one challenged her ability, this work was unmarketable.

She and her husband needed more than her meagre royalties, so she got a job as a producer for the new women's television station in Laramie.

The only problem was that Leah hated her job. She found it humiliating. She was no longer respected for an obscure talent, no longer the centre of attention. Worse, in TV she had to make sense.

As a writer, she could be incomprehensible, and no one would care. In her new job, she was suddenly dependent on her communication skills. Sadder still was that, since it was a women's station, they hired only women. Some of them were lower-class women. Some of them were hard drinking, hard talking, openly sexual, and a bit brutal. Some of them were even lesbians. They were very much like the women she'd written about in her novels.

Leah realized that, though she enjoyed writing novels, and especially prose poems, about such women, she found it nauseating to be exposed to them up close.

To avoid her job, Leah had children.

She loved them dearly, though the process of having them disgusted her. And she knew she could take a year off work in order to have each one. There was no limit to the number of years she could be released with pay. After all, could the new station afford the infamy of having turfed a preeminent novelist because she was with child? Not likely.

When called to the jury, she did her duty. I loved to look at her — she really was a beauty — her head held high, her brown eyes blazing, and her long, straightened, black hair just grazing the top of her stiff, brown back.

Unfortunately, my ugliness, and the sexual details of the trial, caused her verdant poet's brain to imagine complex and exotic scenarios of ritual abuse. Later, in the jury room during deliberations, she'd say, "We must convict him. I will never forget the victims' horror stories. What I found most disgusting was that Klotz would bind his victims with chicken wire. And how could anyone hear how he would dance in the blood of his victims, mix it with his own fecal matter, and then make them eat the congealed mess in order to heighten the possibility of infection, and not be nauseous?"

Unfortunately, none of these details had been related by any — even the most hysterical — witnesses for the prosecution.

The other jurors smiled indulgently. The jury was sequestered for almost a month, and no one dared to challenge Leah on anything.

My Trial

I was afraid of only one witness — Aaron.

It wasn't because I thought he'd prove I was sane. I was banking on that. It would be seeing him up there like that, because of *me*, hearing him talk.

I still wanted Aaron for myself even though I'd wanted to kill him. Looking at him, so frail on the witness stand, I couldn't believe that he'd live very long.

Maybe I'd tried to kill him so that no one else could ever have him.

Silly, right? I've never been monogamous with anyone. Even if I had someone like Aaron waiting for me at home, I'd still be out there every other night having fun, infecting people. Of course, Aaron never had a problem with my promiscuous behaviour. Everything would have been fine if I hadn't been so jealous of that fucking Jeff character.

Actually, my biggest worry was that Aaron would bring up Jeff as a possible reason for my wanting to infect him. I fantasized that Jeff would show up on the day that Aaron took the stand. I remember searching the courtroom for somebody who looked tall and handsome and muscled that day, for a fag who hadn't been there before. Cindy Lou was right, there were no fags in Wyoming. At least no *faggy-looking* fags. That's how crazy jealousy made me. Still. Thank God there wasn't a single, remotely "Jeff-like" person in the whole building.

Aaron's testimony started out okay. I was eager to use Aaron to confirm my trance theory, and sure enough he *fit* it. It was in his bravery. Now, I don't mean to sound as though I'm criticizing someone for being *brave*. But, I suppose, in a way I am. Remember how I said Aaron enjoyed throwing himself into the face of danger, that he wanted to confront it head on? Well, that's precisely what he was doing with this whole AIDS thing. He was facing it bravely and honestly. And he was taking the drugs — the whole kit and caboodle. But he wasn't like Whiny Betty or Nick. And he was beyond Alphonse. He was. . . . You know how they have all those stages of dealing with death and that the final one is "acceptance"? Well, Aaron was already there — with a little unself-conscious bravery thrown in. I watched Leah Johnson during his testimony. She seemed to identify with him. They both held their heads high.

So, yes, Aaron's demeanour supported my trance theory. His was a kind of "heroic" trance. Not in the stupid, sucky, lying way that Whiny Betty was heroic — no, Aaron was a true martyr to AIDS. In a trial that would set precedents as one of the first times that anyone was charged with attempted murder for spreading the AIDS virus, Aaron would be the poster-boy victim. He'd be written up in all the gay mags. Maybe even in *Vanity Fair*. The fact that he was going for it was only more proof of my theory. Aaron wasn't into fame, yet this whole AIDS thing had made him play the martyr.

When he sat down, he looked at me coolly and then never looked at me again. Except once. And it was this look that made all the difference.

They asked him everything I thought they would. About how we met and how we thought we were "in love." And Aaron told them about how I got him drunk one night and that the next week he tested positive for HIV. Of course, he never mentioned his own promiscuity, but I didn't expect him to. No one ever tells the truth about that. And how could I prove that he was promiscuous? Okay, I could have made my attorney ask him about the affair with Jeff, but I didn't want to do that. I didn't want Aaron to even mention Jeff.

But he did.

He talked about his "friendship" with Jeff and my irrational jealousy. He described our fight and my getting him drunk, and he mentioned that he wasn't supposed to drink because of his heart condition.

But what really got to me, the moment that will never go away, was when the prosecuting attorney asked him *the* question. I call it *the* question because it was obviously on everyone's mind. It was the most important point of the trial, actually, the key to every mystery. I mean, they had to ask Aaron how he could even *think* of having sex with someone so ugly. Really, I mean, why do people sleep with people? Why does that beautiful girl go with that ugly old guy? Is it for the money? Does he have a big cock? We need to know.

Now, of course, the prosecuting attorney didn't frame it like that. He had to come off looking like the nice liberal guy who didn't disapprove of Aaron's sexual preferences. So he said, "Now, many of us here in the courtroom don't know the intricacies of what is called the *gay lifestyle.*"

"I'm sure you don't want to know," said Aaron. Which was an intelligent, humorous, good-natured thing to say under the circumstances. It put the jury at ease. Some of them even laughed.

"But what I think many people *might* find hard to understand is, well, frankly, Aaron, you're young, attractive, and at the time you met Kasper were healthy. . . ."

"Well, I wasn't completely healthy," said the always honest Aaron, "I had some illness."

"Okay, okay, but you know what I mean. You're a student, a hard-working kid — a kind, good-looking, young guy. Now, why, for instance, wouldn't you be interested in someone your own age?"

The attorney really wanted to say that I was *ugly*, but he couldn't bring himself to do it. He hoped that Aaron might say it for him.

"Well, Kasper's not that much older than I am."

It was true, I was only ten years older — I just looked like I was one hundred.

"Be that as it may, how shall I put this, well, politely, Aaron, I'm sure you could have any other handsome, hard-working, young student whom you wanted for . . . uh . . . a boyfriend. Now, why would you not choose someone like that for a partner instead of, well, Kasper Klotz?"

And Aaron did the most amazing thing then and lived up to the kindness in his eyes. He looked at me, very compassionately, and then turned, quite honestly and innocently, to the prosecuting attorney. "What are you trying to say?" he asked.

"Well," said the state's representative, embarrassed, "I mean — "

"Are you saying that you think Kasper is ugly?"

"Well, of course I'm not saying that. But it's certainly true that he's not — "

"Oh, no," said Aaron. "How can you say that? Kasper is not ugly. He is very attractive. I'm sure that some people don't find him attractive. But everyone has different romantic tastes. And, you know, I even think he's got an ugliness complex. In fact, I think that's one of his problems. That's what might have led to all this. He was so irrationally jealous of my friend — Jeff. But he never had anything to be jealous about. I think Kasper Klotz is a very beautiful man."

Before his little speech was over, I melted inside. Yes, Kasper's cold heart melted. It was the beginning of another revelation.

That night I went back to my cell and was so inspired that I wrote pages and pages of my defence speech. I even wrote a letter to Cindy Lou. I finally, truly understood how pervasive our trances were, how easy it was to be trapped by them.

You can be caught up in many trances. And if you can break through one, then you can break through them all. Only then can you be free.

The trance that I have always lived in? That I'm ugly.

Aaron had broken through it.

Kasper Klotz would be ugly no more.

Letter from Kasper Klotz to Cindy Lou

Cindy Lou, baby,

Hey. Cindy Lou. Here I am for you. Cindy Lou. I love you. Cindy Lou Who. What's up, Cindy Lou?

So, you hate me now. That is utterly too badsville. Pardon me, but today came unto me the revelation of revelations. That moment. When you know. Know the truth. Truth sublime. It's like wine. Cindy Lou. I have to share it with you.

HEY, WE HAVE BEEN SEPARATE BUT LIKE TOGETHER? WE HAVE BEEN TOTALLY APART BUT SOMEHOW CONNECTED (AT THE HIP?). WE HAVE BEEN ENEMIES BUT SOMEHOW FRIENDS, AND THAT'S BECAUSE, THAT'S BECAUSE. WE'RE BOTH UGLY.

but we're not. please don't stop reading here cindylou because this is the most important moment of our lives a time to break out and be free to not be "inside" of it but instead "outside" if you know what eye mean break thru cindy lou to the other side where the grass is green and you are not fat and you are not ugly and you may still have limp and lifeless hair but it doesn't matter don't you sea? it is free you may give yourself the permission to be beautiful we may all do that who says: who says we are ugly? my boy aaron my boy says eye'm beautiful so eye am and so can you be too. not just in his eyes or my eyes but in your own eye. oh my god cindy lou go ahead put your hands down there feel is that not your own cunt and is it not warm and wet and good and who says who says they don't want to go there put your hand down there feel and it's okay yeah it's okay for you to be like that too. never mind cindy lou. mother's sleeping. the eye the other eye that isn't your eye is closed. only your eye exists. breathe with it.

What I was trying to say with the above, Cindy Lou, babe, just in case you didn't *get* it, is that I was in a trance all these years. I thought I looked like this:

Quasimodo. I know it's crazy. But now I know I don't look like that. Maybe I look like this:

Maybe it's an exaggeration too. Maybe I'm somewhere in between. But I am beautiful and human, and I'm no longer caught in the trance that says I'm not. I have stepped out. You can step out too. Just lift your hand. Peer through the curtain. No, they're not out there ready to laugh at you. And if they do, so what? Maybe it's a comedy.

eye implore you to stop being cindy boo hoo loo and be cynthia whether that's your real name or not you are beautiful cindy lou and eye am too

sincerely, from one who taught you how to hate but gee whiz come on forget all that

Kasper

Eighth Prison Letter from Cindy Lou Williams

Dearest Kasper,

Now I can say these words to you. Now I feel comfortable with them. Now you are my Dearest Kasper.

Dearest. Let me say it again. Dearest. I have read your letter over and over. And despite its strange punctuation and unneces-sary profanity, I think that there is a kind of poetry there. A kind of modern poetry. Something sings in your letter, Dearest Kasper! It sings for me, and you have to understand that no one has ever sung for me before!

I understand now. I understand that I was right. As much as you deny it; Dearest Kasper, as much as you deny your "hetero-sexuality," as you call it, your last letter can be nothing less than an admission of love.

What care we for labels? What care we for trials? What care we for prisons and laws and persecution? I know that you could not have attempted to kill that boy. A man like you, with the soul of an artist, is not capable of such horror.

I accept that you might be mentally unbalanced. And I know today, now that the prosecution rests, that the cards are stacked against you. What will you say on the stand? How will you turn the tide?

I have faith in your mind and your heart, my Dearest. When they set you free, I will be waiting.

Excuse me for the change in tone. And the change in hand-writing. I was interrupted by my mother, who found the rare energy to surprise me in my own room. I told her to go away.

I told my mother to go away! Do you realize what that entails?

I await with bated breath your speech and your acquittal. Love and Kisses

    your dearest Cynthia

The Private Life of Juror 10

His name was Henry Makepeace, but to his friends he was Hank.

Don't get me wrong. He didn't try to hide his homosexuality. Everyone knew. But they didn't. . . .

There was nothing flamboyant or effeminate about Hank. *But* he lived in a house with another man — a house that they'd *decorated* together. *And* the house had been restored in authentic nineteenth-century High Tiffany, correct in every detail. *And* he wasn't married. *But* he walked like a cowboy. *But* he never claimed to be a heterosexual. *But* he never denied being gay.

Hey, it never came up. Why would it? His lover was a doctor. They kept dogs.

Sure, Hank sold antiques for a living. *But* he wasn't one of *those* antique dealers.

He was on every committee in Kasper. For the improvement of everything.

He never held the arm of his lover in public. *But* his lover was always there. Because he was on all the committees too.

A gay-libber would have a hard time arguing with Hank Makepeace. He was living his gay life, yet it wasn't an issue because it wasn't really a "gay" life. At least not in the traditional sense.

Can I tell you something? Something that really makes me mad?

Hank had *everything* to do with what happened to me. He had *everything* to do with the verdict. Hank wouldn't rest until I was put away. Why? Because this trial was a threat to his life in Kasper. If Hank was to remain "Hank" and not "Henry" — you know, glasses, carries-a-briefcase, skinny, make-fun-of, beat-him-up Henry — then I had to be convicted of *something*.

Look at it from Hank's point of view.

Hank spends his whole life working at surviving in a small town by being the most respectable homosexual who's ever lived.

And it's working. Like a dream. And suddenly fate puts him on a jury that is judging an ugly — or what deluded people, not Aaron and I and Cindy Lou, see as ugly — promiscuous, AIDS-infected fag. Hank knew that if I were to get off, then it would inevitably blow his cover. Everyone would assume that one homo got the other off. Everyone would assume, if I were to be deemed innocent, that it was Hank's doing. Hank would then be just Henry, another faggot. And more than anything in the world, Hank did not want to be Henry. So, for everything that happened, Hank is responsible.

But you know what? To me, he'll always be Henry. A fucking faggot.

My Speech

Many thousands of years ago, a cave man looked different from his brothers. He was born with a strawberry birthmark across his face. When he reached the age of puberty, he was stripped and hung upside down from a tree. His cave-dwelling sisters and brothers taunted him and laughed. Then they ran away in fear. And then, in order to deal with their own fear of minor, perceived differences and imperfections, in order to quell their primeval self-hatred, they returned and threw stones at him until there was nothing left of the innocent being but inert, bloody, dangling flesh.

This was the first scapegoat.

In the Middle Ages, it was commonly held that leprosy was the result of impurity. It was thought to be caused by *the filth of lechery* or *the conception of a child in menstrual time*. People believed it was spread by having sexual intercourse with a woman who'd been intimate with a leper. The disease of the lepers, its consequent disfiguration, was so disgusting, and considered so contagious, that lepers were shipped to remote islands, where only the bravest doctors and clerics dared to venture. Today we know that leprosy is not contagious, that it is not blood or semen borne, and that it can be successfully treated.

The historical treatment of lepers will always stand as a testament to hate and ignorance, a warning against the human need to make pariahs of the diseased.

In Papua New Guinea, the ritual process of "shaming" is delivered through a harangue. The scapegoated individual, who's been selected because of a perceived transgression against a clan taboo, sits silently inside his or her house. All of the town listens in silence to the harangue as it is shouted into the night. The shamed individual understands that the whole town has heard his or her humiliation. The infamy is so great that sometimes the shamed will commit suicide by jumping from a palm tree. For some, the only release from pain is death.

In this way, we begin to see that historically scapegoats — out of desperation, ignorance, and loneliness — can often be burdened with so much guilt that they actively seek their own deaths.

In the late nineteenth century and early twentieth century, Jews were persecuted throughout Europe. This led to the popularity of the Nazi, Hitler, who rose to power on a platform of hatred and scapegoating. It was in the cold heart of the Jew, Hitler said, that all of the evils of the world originated. The Germans were acting not *like Germans* but *like typical humans* when they eagerly shamed the blameless Jew. The Jew, as is always the case with the historical scapegoat, took on all the oppressors' sins and left the German gentiles free of fear but full of hate.

Some Jews, it has been reported, walked dutifully to the ovens, accepting a martyr's death, others collaborated with their oppressors. And why not? Compliance becomes a natural release when scapegoating reaches such institutionalized intensity.

Each era and culture has had its own pariah. Humans are necessarily creatures of guilt and fear. The primary way of dealing with these feelings is projection. Disease, violence, indeed sin and evil themselves, come from elsewhere, from someone else, from another country. *We* are never the origin.

When I was eight years old, I adored my best friend, Trent Atwater. He was perfect in every way: beautiful, smart, and athletic. His mother was an artist, and his father was a psychologist. Trent and his sister, Melinda, were allowed to stay up late and watch the terrifying TV show *The Outer Limits*. I wasn't allowed to stay up late and was allowed to watch only a much tamer show, *The Twilight Zone*. Dinner-table discussion at the Atwaters was free and sometimes contentious, almost violent. Discussion at our house was limited to the weather and the most wholesome news items; we passed the iodized salt and made sure not to put our elbows on the table. The Atwaters had a trampoline in their backyard. We were allowed only a shallow plastic wading pool. Breakfast at the Atwaters was a merry affair; they often consumed delectable English muffins dripping in butter. At my house, Mother would only prepare toast with a thin scraping of margarine. I remember whining to my grandmother once, on one of her rare visits, "Nannie, why can't we have English muffins dripping with butter like the Atwaters?" Nannie was quick and unapologetic with her shaming, scapegoating answer: "Don't worry, let them have what they like for breakfast," she said, "those Atwaters won't live long."

More than forty years later, Trent Atwater is a prominent psychologist; he has followed in the footsteps of his esteemed father. His sister, Melinda, married a baron. They were recently divorced, but she has made ends meet by opening a lucrative floral-and-basket-design business in Niagara Falls. The elder Atwaters, their parents, are still as vocal as ever and still find time to "trampoline" after eating greasy English muffins and catching eternal reruns of *The Outer Limits*.

Why was it that my nannie couldn't give me an honest answer?

Why couldn't she just have said, "Well, that's the way the Atwaters do it. Here we just have margarine and toast"? I'll tell you why. Because the Atwaters were different, and that was very threatening.

Why can't humans acknowledge difference and the possibility that others might enjoy their lives differently? Have different customs, foods, ways of making love, whatever? Why does difference always have to be condemned?

Because we are threatened by difference.

Sometimes I think that humans were meant only to live in small villages, isolated from each other, with no knowledge of a stranger's customs. It seems that when we *are* exposed to difference our natural impulse is to draw a sword.

The other reason behind my nannie's answer was, quite simply, this: the Atwaters were having more fun. This is where the threat really came from. The only way to counter my jealous longing for juicy, dripping English muffins was to poison them, to position the Atwaters as pariahs. Then, by golly, *this* little boy would dream of English muffins no more.

It didn't work. As soon as I moved out, the first thing I did was buy myself a big pack of English muffins and a pound of butter. I ate nothing else for quite a few months after that. There were still requisite tugs of guilt, of course. Sometimes, during that period, I would wake up in the middle of the night and feel my pulse to make sure that my heart was still beating.

But why would I bring up the seemingly trivial finger wagging of my grandmother when I am being tried for attempted murder?

Because it is my contention that it wasn't possible for me to kill Aaron Bucolic, or anyone else, with my supposedly lethal semen. Because I do not believe that my semen, in and of itself, is lethal. I do not believe, ladies and gentlemen, that AIDS is a purely physical disease — though I don't deny that there are certainly physical elements to it. Instead, it is my contention that AIDS is an institutionalized ritual, the public shaming of the scapegoat. Who is doing the shaming? The Christian right. And who is the scapegoat? The homosexual, the drug addict, the prostitute, the black. And what are these people dying of if it isn't a physical condition? My theory is that AIDS is a form of masked depression, as utterly psychological as a case of mass hysteria. The relatively unmined but potent field of psychohistory tells us that people can die because *they believe they must.*

The Private Life of the Prosecuting Attorney

Craig Woods was almost five foot nine, but that didn't stop him.

Craig was a sportsman; every weekend he'd take his children hunting. If the kids mishandled the gun, he'd get really upset. After all, guns are dangerous things. You've got to be careful. The funniest thing was when he gave his son's friend, Walter, the elephant gun to try. Boy, that was a riot. The kick of the thing practically tossed the kid across the large field. Walter's little glasses flew off too, and that was also funny.

Craig was also very serious about the American flag. Once, his youngest kid, Franklin, let one touch the ground. This is what Craig said to him: **"GIVE ME THAT! GIVE IT TO ME! I SAID GIVE IT TO ME! DON'T YOU EVER, DO YOU HEAR ME? EVER! LET THAT FLAG TOUCH THE GROUND AGAIN. DO YOU KNOW WHAT THIS IS? LOOK AT ME! DON'T LOOK AT THE GROUND! I SAID LOOK AT ME! DON'T YOU EVER, EVER LET THAT FLAG TOUCH THE GROUND! DO YOU REALIZE WHAT THIS FLAG REPRESENTS? DO YOU REALIZE WHAT THIS FLAG MEANS? DO YOU REALIZE THAT YOUR DAD FOUGHT IN KOREA TO SAVE THIS FLAG AND THIS COUNTRY? DO YOU KNOW WHAT IT MEANS WHEN YOU LET THIS FLAG TOUCH THE GROUND? ANSWER ME! ANSWER ME! IT MEANS THAT YOU SPIT ON YOUR FATHER! IS THAT WHAT YOU**

WANT TO DO? DO YOU WANT TO SPIT ON YOUR FATHER? IS THAT WHAT YOU WANT? WHY, YOU LITTLE. . . . " Little Franklin was sure sorry he'd let that flag touch the ground.

Actually, little Franklin was often sorry.

Craig was a *registered psychotic*. Yes. Registered, in the sense that he had a little card that said he was registered with the right people. As a consequence, he wasn't allowed to drive a car. Cars agitated him. So every morning you'd see the short, muscular, handsome Craig Woods riding to the legal offices of Woods, Woods, and Bethany on his red bicycle, his short, cropped, reddish-brown bush of hair never moving in the wind.

Craig wasn't supposed to have guns. He wasn't even supposed to get married, but he did. He beat his wife, June, regularly. But she loved Craig, his masterful tight body, his prodigious sexual appetite. And they always made up.

Sometimes it was hard to hide the bruises, though.

The problem was that, occasionally, Craig beat the children. When they handled guns improperly, for instance, or when they dropped the flag.

For the most part, Craig obeyed all the laws of the land. At least he never got caught. He obeyed the traffic signals when he rode his bike. When he worked for the DA, he was a dedicated, in fact diligent, prosecutor. They used to call him "Bulldog."

It's true, you know. He was a good prosecutor. But I'm glad I never had to spend any time alone with him.

My Speech

I am accused of attempting to murder Aaron Bucolic with infected semen. But this is impossible. Would you put a man in jail for attacking someone with a wet noodle? No. I am not making a sexual pun, for my lovemaking wasn't lacking in virility. Yes, I spilled my seed in Aaron's rectum. But that alone cannot kill Aaron. Why?

Well, here's a question for you. If Aaron is now living under my anally inserted death sentence, then I must be infected, correct? Why, then, am *I* not dead?

It is said that I am HIV positive and that I am going to die of AIDS. Really? What's taking so long? I, like thousands and thousands of other men, was given my death sentence in 1982. At the time, I was diagnosed with GRID, what was then called "gay-related immune deficiency." Interesting, isn't it, that this was once the "gay disease." And though the name has been changed to be politically correct, it is still the "gay disease" and always will be the "gay disease." It is the disease of pariahs, of scapegoats. It is a disease of "the hated." In 1982, my doctor told me to get my papers in order, that I would soon be getting the horrible marks of Kaposi's sarcoma: the mark of Cain, the mark of evil, the mark of the monkey, the mark of the deadly "gay disease." Naturally, there was much tongue wagging and disapproval of the lifestyle that would lead to my death, a death that would occur in short order.

It is now 1999. That is almost eighteen years ago. I have not died. *I have not even been ill.* The odd cold, that's it. True, every time I go to a hospital and a doctor finds out about my diagnosis — I've stopped telling them for this reason — they want to put me on AZT or a protease inhibitor or whatever lethal drug is in fashion. But I will never take those heavy-duty, chemotherapy drugs. Every person I know who's taken those drugs has died. I talked to a homeopath who told me that taking AZT for AIDS is the equivalent of using an atom bomb to clear crabgrass. Sure, doctors take my so-called T-cell count and tell me I have only months left. But nothing ever happens. All is the same with me.

So, is this so-called disease lethal? When they found the virus that's supposed to cause this thing, they said that most people who had it would die. Then, when people like me continued to live, they said people might live for eight years. Then, when people like me lived longer, they said, "Well, people with AIDS might live for ten or twelve years." Now that I won't die, that I refuse to die, and others like me are the same, they say, "People with AIDS may live for fifteen or twenty years." When does this lunacy stop? How long can they stretch the goal posts before the cat is out of the bag? If I dic in a car accident, will they say that AIDS finally got me?

Yes, there are many like me. Everywhere I turn I meet a long-term survivor. They like to be called "thrivers" now. We have no idea how many survivors of HIV there are, because *they only test the sick ones.* So you know why you're hearing this today? Only because I'm on trial for attempted murder. If I wasn't, do you think I'd mention that I'm HIV positive? Why should I? It hasn't made a speck of difference in my life.

In the gay community, it's the unspoken secret. If you're a long-term survivor, you're a disgrace to the dead. It's a blot on the memory of those who have died for me to live and thrive and be happy. But I'm telling you that I live and thrive so that others may live.

Consider what happens to rats when you trap and repeatedly shock them. When rodents are exposed to inescapable electrical impulses, they develop what is called "learned helplessness." The result? Weight loss and *loss of cell immunity.*

The psychological and political weaponry of the Christian right is our human, cultural equivalent of inescapable shock. For the previous generation, it was Anita Bryant, just as today it's Reverend Phelps and his godhatesfags.com sitting hatefully inside our rabid culture. Oh, you may say, "They're just the extremists. Most people have pity for AIDS victims. Most people love AIDS victims." But don't you see how that's the same thing? Don't you see that gays have always been considered sick? At one time, a hundred years ago, we were physically sick. Then, in the 1940s and 1950s, we were mentally sick. Now we're physically sick again. No, in your liberal pity and concern, there is an underlying hatred. I'm not saying that you want to hate us or that, in the case of some well-meaning liberals, you actually do hate us; still, the disgust you feel when faced with our gay lifestyle, when asked to consider gay sexual acts, is *inside the culture.* Behind everything. It's in every gay joke. You know, I used to like those AIDS jokes. I used to tell them to people when I thought I was killing them. Go ahead now, call me politically correct; I finally realize they're just a symptom of hate. When I told them, it was a symptom of my self-hatred. You see, behind every social blunder is hate: "Excuse me, what should I call him . . . your lover . . . I mean . . . since you're two men, he's not really your husband, is he?" All very well meaning, indeed. But still a hatred of difference, of the demon other. I used to relish being evil. I never knew why, that's just the way I used to be. Now I know that I relished it because everybody always told me I was evil and ugly. Today I don't believe it.

What do you think happens to a group of people when they are reminded, repeatedly, that they are evil and deserve to die? When their families cast them from homes and insist they don't love them anymore? What do you suppose happens to a group of people when we remove society's love, support, and approval?

They wither and die.

I am not saying that AIDS has no physical manifestations. I'm sure there are physiological changes that have nothing to do with mass depression. But I am saying that no one could possibly thrive in a culture that, deep down, wants him or her to die.

You may not believe that what I say is possible. But newly researched psychohistory tells us otherwise. There are countless documented cases of mass hysteria, human epidemics, including what's known as the June Bug Epidemic as well as the case of The Phantom Gasser. Still other unexplainable epidemics have recently occurred in the Far East. All are documented. I have read about them, and you can read about them too. These were real epidemics in which many people fell ill and sometimes died. There were terrible physical symptoms for which experts could find little or no organic justification. There were quite obvious mental reasons, however. Stress, the power of suggestion, a kind of mass hypnosis. Yes, there is such a thing as mass hysteria. And, no, we don't know enough about it; more information is needed, more research. Because we are in the middle of a huge epidemic of mass hysteria now.

If Aaron Bucolic dies, then it has nothing to do with my puny, infected semen. Rather, it has everything to do with the fact that he lives in a society that denies his humanity and his right to life. It is because he encounters hatred, both veiled and obvious, almost every day. It is because we are all in a trance. And in that trance, the homosexual takes on all the sins of society, all its mistakes, all the guilt, all the pain. This is a trance of punishment and redemption. Of guilt and release. We are your sexual ones, your evil ones, your perverted ones. You hated these things in yourselves, so you found someone to punish.

Us.

You tell me that what I have is a physical disease and that it's not in any way related to a sociological or psychological condition. But when I turn on my television, and a promiscuous teenage girl sits in the hotseat on *The Maury Povich Show* or *The Sally Jessy Raphael Show*, I see the ugly faces, contorted in hate. Hear the voices of the audience yelling "You know what will happen to you. You'll die of AIDS, you slut! You deserve to die of AIDS!" I used to enjoy those programs. Once they were actually my favourite TV shows. But now I also see the joy and relief on these faces that go with those voices when they have released their venom.

It makes sense. The fags are your martyrs. We are your release. We are where your evil comes to rest.

No one knows if Aaron Bucolic will actually die of AIDS. If he does, then he is certainly not to blame. But neither am I. I have always been a homosexual who hates himself. This is something

I just discovered because of the love I saw in someone's eyes. How can I not be? Aaron is a homosexual who hates himself. How can Aaron not be? How can we not hate our own kind when society constantly tells us how evil we are? All homosexuals hate themselves somewhere inside. We exist in a trance. So, if Aaron dies, then there is no single individual to blame. But there is blame to be laid: on a society that has shamed him, that has made it nearly impossible for him to live with his head held high, that has even made the spectre of AIDS and death more attractive than the constant, never-ending battle to sustain self-esteem in a homophobic world.

Look at my so-called victims. Look at the homosexuals who have come before you. One of them thanked me for changing his life! Another's never been sick a day in his life and is obviously revelling in his pending martyrdom. Another is clearly crazy, he believes he's related to Czar Nicholas II. The prosecution forgot to mention that. Can you see that his relationship to Russian aristocracy and his claim to be infected by this disease are similar? That both are delusions? Can you see that they all hate themselves, that they're in an AIDS trance?

Convict me of attempted murder and you buy into a paradigm that is based on a myth.

You may be tempted to call me a conspiracy theorist. To say that I see a hobgoblin behind every door.

Yes, I do.

But I do not see a conspiracy here. I do not think that Anita Bryant, or Reverend Phelps, or your Dear Aunt Minna, who hates homosexuals and can't even say the word, are to blame. They, too, are victims of a human failing, just as the Nazis were victims. Just as those who persecuted lepers were victims. Homophobes are victims of their own fear. Victims of an institutionalized hatred that we must *somehow* change.

How? You can start, here, by setting me free and admitting that

AIDS is more than a physical disease. That the issue is more complex than many are willing to accept. That AIDS is, in fact, a disease of society, not of the individual, a disease created and spread in hate.

I know. I hated those I thought I was killing. But I could not kill them. I alone could not kill them with my stupid prick, no matter how hard I tried.

If you're so sure I'm going to die a horrible death, if you're so sure I have a fatal disease, then why put me in jail? If you really believe I'm a murderer, then you'll be content to let this horrible disease be my punishment. But here I am, alive and kicking. If you put me in jail, then that's admitting you think I will remain healthy long enough to infect more people. Don't you see the contradiction?

But if you set me free, you may start wheels in motion that will set us all free. Can you imagine a world without hate?

I can.

Because the hate is not just in Kasper. The hate is in the world.

The Private Life of the Judge

Elmer Cranshaw was one of the most respected judges in Wyoming. He'd rendered fair and judicial judgement in many cases, weighing the evidence and arguments, never allowing emotion to sway reason.

I remember looking up at him and wishing, though, that he had a more kindly face.

Elmer's face was not kindly. It was pinched and unhappy. His lips were always pursed in a kind of schoolmarmish way.

When Elmer spoke, words escaped from his old lady's lips as if they were so much hot, tired, infected air.

Elmer had the face of a pervert. And by that, I mean a pervert in the old, classical sense. I mean, some people might consider me perverted. But the *classical* pervert is someone with a very secret, very vile sex life.

You see, once a month Elmer would slip off to Las Vegas. "I've got the gambling bug!" he'd say to appease his curious friends — he had no wife or immediate family.

In Las Vegas, he'd get very drunk and invite hookers into his luxurious suite, always on the last night of his stay. They'd squat over his old lady's face, and he'd say, "Go ahead, darling, let it go, let it all go." Then they'd pee all over him.

Elmer would lie there like a flabby, old, wet puddle. He wouldn't lick, or make noise, or say, "Do it to me, baby!" He'd just lie there.

The money was always on the table by the door.

When he went home, Elmer always had a headache, and he'd complain that he'd lost too much money gambling. But he'd sigh, as he sank into a chair at the exclusive men's club to which he belonged, and say, "It's my one vice, you know."

Like all perverts, Judge Elmer Cranshaw couldn't look at me.

My Trial

I suppose you want to know what happened. Something pretty unexpected, actually. At least it was to me. It seemed to make perfect sense to everyone else.

I got off. That is, they didn't put me in jail. But they put me in the loony bin. Oh yeah, I'm here with the loonies.

Maybe you expected it. When you read my speech, you probably thought, "This guy is nuts!" Well, I didn't think I was nuts when I wrote it. In fact, I still believe in all that shit. I do. That's what keeps me in here.

There was some dissent on the jury, though.

The Private Life of Jurors 11 and 12

Maisie Lee Hicks and Lincoln Alexander. Wow.

How sweet it is to have supporters. They lost, though. Just couldn't take it.

Maisie was a really nice old lady. She was about sixty-five but had physical problems that made her feel more like seventy-five. Bad circulation due to the diabetes. She wasn't *well*.

Lincoln was a young black juror who was just, well, smarter than everybody else. Except for Maisie. The two of them bonded, but the opposition was so overwhelming that they gave up.

Maisie kept saying, "It doesn't make sense. The part of Kasper's speech that really got to me was when he said, 'Let my disease be my punishment.' And when he talked about living for eighteen years and still being healthy, I mean, what *is* this disease we're talking about? I had no idea there were people with AIDS who don't get *sick*. And that crazy man who was so obsessed with Rachmaninoff and so obsessed with having AIDS? There's something wrong here. It just doesn't make sense. Shouldn't some of these victims be tested for AIDS? Isn't that what you'd call reasonable doubt?"

Maisie would say these things at least once every day during their weeks of deliberation. She drove everyone crazy. Both Lorena Mady Kelly and Hank Makepeace wanted to kill her. They all said, in fact, that if Maisie Lee Hicks hadn't been so damned stubborn they would have been out of there in a day rather than a month.

Lincoln Alexander was much younger than Maisie, one of two black people on the jury, and more easily intimidated than she was. He kept his ideas to himself. He understood the frustration the other jurors felt about Maisie. He was getting frustrated himself. He had a wife and a new little girl at home.

There were parts of my speech that made a lot of sense to him. "What about all those black men in prison?" Lincoln thought.

"Didn't the white men put them there? Or is that just a conspiracy theory, too, just like Kasper's ideas?"

He sided with Maisie for acquittal. But he began to feel that he was becoming a pariah. If he didn't agree that I was insane, then the rest of the jury thought *he* was nuts. Lincoln wasn't about to endure ten white people thinking he was nuts.

Maisie held out for four long weeks. But then her health began to give way, and her sister, Darla, sat her down and had a talk with her. "Maisie," she said, "you're killing yourself over this verdict. You just don't have the health. Do yourself and all of us a favour. Put the guy away, will you?" And so she gave in.

It was nice to know that two out of twelve didn't think I was nuts, though. Not that I really care.

The End

So that's basically it. They locked me up and threw away the key. I don't mind. Actually, that's not the truth. They have me under constant observation. And sure, if I said the right things, I know they'd let me out.

For instance, if I said that I had AIDS, and that AIDS was going to kill me, and that AIDS is a purely physiological, infectious disease, then they'd release me for sure. If I said that my big speech was wrong. If I said that people don't really hate fags that much, then I know I could get out. If I said that there is no "conspiracy" and that the world is a pretty nice place, then they'd think I was ready for the world.

The hardest thing for me to say, though, is that people don't hate fags. Because I still think people do.

I certainly changed when Aaron said that nice thing about me on the witness stand. Ever since, I've been trying to live up to his expectations. I've been trying to live up to his eyes.

They still let me write. But they take it and analyse it, of course. As for my social life, there's one night nurse here who is gay. He sucks me off now and then. He's sort of an Aaron type. Every so often I look out the window and think about Aaron and about what he said. Then I feel pretty good for a while. I amuse myself sometimes by drawing pictures of how I think I might really look. The doctors seem to like that. It keeps them thinking I'm loony.

"Why don't you just look in a mirror?" they ask.

I don't know how to explain to those doctors that a mirror doesn't tell you the truth.

Of course, they try to give me the AIDS pills. I pretend to take them, but then I spit them out. They keep talking about something called "enforced medication": they sit you in a room and watch you take your pills.

Oh yeah, I forgot. I still get crazy letters from Cindy Lou.

Hospital Letter from Cindy Lou

Dearest Kasper,

I miss you terribly. I still hope that you will say whatever they ask you to say so they will let you out.

I don't believe those stories about the night nurse. Why do you keep telling me those things? You know I don't believe them.

I keep your "poetical" letter by my bedside and read it every night, though I have crossed out the one offensive sentence.

I have written a short prose poem which I hope you will enjoy. Although I am not a writer, like you, I think that it expresses *something*.

Kasper, you are my shining star. You are someone who understands what. What I mean. The world is mean to you and to me. To both of us. But we know about beauty and what it is. I can feel you holding my hand, Kasper. I feel that if you ever . . . I cannot write the words, but . . . suffice it to say . . . whatever. Whatever you want to give to me, I will receive it. And I will believe that it is pure. Please give it to me, Kasper. Give. It. To. Me. Please.

I've read my little poem over and over, and I don't really know what it means. I suppose that it's "in the abstract."

I love you dearly, Kasper. You are the only person who truly understands me and what it's like to be "out of the ordinary." I am going to come to visit you as soon as you are ready. I know that you will be ready some day real soon.

Keep that pretty chin of yours up, mister. I believe that you're sane, for whatever it's worth!

Yours,
Cynthia

Oh, I Forgot

I guess I'll sign off now. Until the next instalment.

Wait, I forgot one thing. I forgot to tell you about Aaron. I was going to tell you, but I got wrapped up in writing about myself.

He died. Yeah. It was very upsetting at first. They found his dead body one morning tied to a fencepost in a field near Laramie. Some gay-basher types. Probably some rough-looking guy he thought he'd flirt with. Aaron was always testing himself.

Oh well.

At first, I was relieved. I thought, "Wow, he didn't die of AIDS. After my trial, and my getting put away, and everything. Wow, AIDS didn't get him!" That almost made me feel better. You know, that he didn't die from AIDS, that he died from gay-bashing. But then it occurred to me: they're kind of the same thing. At least they are if you're willing to look at things a bit differently.

Appendix: Kasper's Confession

Yeah, I killed a lot of people. A lot of boring, useless drag queens and dumb homosexuals who were just taking up space anyway.

I killed a drag queen once named Elvita because she had a stupid argument with a friend of mine. My friend is this lovely, sweet drag queen named Misty. Much lovelier than Elvita, who was big and ham-handed and couldn't lip-synch within an inch of her life.

Well, one night lovely Misty was supposed to do this little public service announcement for safe sex in the parks at our local bar, Stiffy's. When she arrived, she had to fix her makeup, so she asked the manager if there was a dressing room. The manager said, "Sure, there's a little dressing room downstairs." He neglected to mention that Elvita was already in it.

Well, anyway, down Misty goes and opens the door to what she figures is the dressing room. And Elvita is standing there in the altogether. That's a pretty horrifying sight, I can tell you. And Elvita goes nuts. Nuts with pretension. She starts yelling at Misty, "Get out of here, get out of here, you slut! This is *my* dressing room! Get out of here. Leave. Leave now! This is a *private* dressing room. Get the fuck out!" And then she pushes Misty, and Misty falls. And Elvita continues yelling: "Oh, don't try to fake it, you pitiful bitch, I didn't push you that hard!" So Misty ends up staggering out of Stiffy's in severe pain, and with a bruised hip, and almost doesn't make it home.

She never got to deliver her safe-sex-in-the-parks message. Not that it would have helped anybody. Who wants a message about safe sex in the parks? You go there to get dirty and fucked up, give me a break.

Anyway, when I heard about all this, it really pissed me off. Mainly because there wasn't an actual dressing room to get mad about. Everyone knew very well that Elvita put on her makeup in

Stiffy's broom closet. So there she was, being all pretentious and angry and protective and like a mother lion guarding her cubs, over what? There was something about Elvita having the gall and stupidity to knock my friend Misty onto the floor for the sake of defending *a broom closet* that made me very angry.

So I killed her. I killed Elvita because she was stupid and pretentious and tried to defend a broom closet.

And I tried to kill a beautiful boy once because he was just too beautiful.

But before I tell you about that, I want to tell you about how I killed this horrible guy at the baths because he tried to trick me into having unsafe sex. What a creep. I mean, not that I haven't used the same trick on hundreds of guys. But please, honey, please don't try it on me. He was fucking me up the ass, and then he pulled out for some reason. I happened to look back, and he was *taking off the condom* and reinserting his prick. Well, thank God he didn't see me catch him at it. But I didn't care. I just let him go ahead and fuck me and come.

And then I told him I wanted to fuck him. And then I put on a condom that I deliberately broke and fucked him good and hard. Just as I was coming, I yelled, "Sorry, the condom's broken, and I've got AIDS! Here's some positive joyjuice, baby!"

It was fabulous. He squirmed around like crazy trying to get out from underneath me. It completely enhanced my orgasm. Boy, was that guy mad! When he finally got out from under me, I waved the broken, semeny condom in his face so he could see that I'd really infected him. I thought he was going to punch me. But he was too middle class for that. He just marched out of the room all red in the face.

Actually, I killed him mainly because he was a real estate agent. Have you ever met any of those gay real estate agents? Their big thing is how respectable and responsible they are. And what great citizens they are. They put their pictures in the gay papers to say

"I'm a gay real estate agent and proud of it." Ugh. Always wearing suits. Those kind of fags really piss me off, you know?

I killed the mailman because he never used to bring me my mail on time. He was kind of a greasy, skinny guy mainly into water sports. But he had a big dick, so he was fun. I fucked him one night in an alley and left a note in his pocket. I used to carry these little notes, kind of like calling cards, that said "Tag, you're it." He knew what it meant. He had a nervous breakdown and had to stop delivering mail. The new mailman was much better.

And, yeah, I attempted to kill Aaron Bucolic. If I'd killed him, they wouldn't have been able to bring this suit against me.

I tried to kill Aaron because. . . .

Why should I tell you?

I decided . . . well, I guess I sort of told you about him before. He was the one who, I decided . . . fuck, why can't I say it?

I guess it's remorse. I must be feeling remorse. I've never felt remorse before. It feels weird.

Yeah, well, I tried to kill him because he was too beautiful to live.

I don't mean pretty. Lots of people are pretty. Big deal. Let 'em live. I'm talking about someone who's just too *nice* to live. No, I don't really mean nice, I mean . . . the fuzz on a dove's tail. That's what he was. Have you ever put your hand on a dove's back? The body of the bird quivers a little, as if it's crying. And there's a bit of fuzz there on the white of the tail.

Aaron had to die because he was the fuzz on a dove's tail.

And the world . . . you know? It's filled with fucking pigeons.

So I did it for his sake. Because we didn't deserve him.

Writer, filmmaker, director, or drag queen extraordinaire, Sky Gilbert is one of North America's most controversial artistic forces. Born in Norwich, Connecticut in 1952, he made Toronto his home in 1965. He was co-founder and artistic director of Buddies in Bad Times Theatre for 18 years where his award-winning plays included *Suzy Goo: Private Secretary* and *The Whore's Revenge*. His new AIDS-radical play, *The Birth of Casper G. Schmidt* will tour the USA in 2002. His third feature film, *My Summer Vacation* was recently released (by Waterbearer Films) to video stores in the USA and Canada. ECW Press published his first full-length collection of poetry, *Digressions of a Naked Party Girl* in 1998, and his memoir *Ejaculations From The Charm Factory* in 2000. His first two novels: *Guilty* and *St. Stephen's* were critically acclaimed. He is presently writing his fourth novel and working towards a Ph.D. in Drama at The University of Toronto.